The LAWLESS OZARKS

CC BROWN

Publishing Coordinator & Book Design
Sharon Kizziah-Holmes
Cover Design – Jaycee DeLorenzo

an imprint of Paperback Press, LLC
Springfield, Missouri

ISBN -13: 978-1-970560-19-0

THE LAWLESS OZARKS

1855-1890

The Ozark Mountain region, commonly referred to by the locals as "the Ozarks," includes portions of Kansas, Missouri, Arkansas, and Oklahoma. Key historical events had a significant impact on the lives of people living in the four-state area.

1855-Kansas Border Wars

The Border Wars, also known as "Bleeding Kansas" and "Bloody Kansas," were a series of violent confrontations between settlers and pro-slavery "border ruffians." The central question of the conflict was whether the Kansas Territory would permit or prohibit slavery, thereby entering the Union as either a slave state or a free state.

1856 to 1896-The Great Cattle Drives

Cattle drives were a major economic activity in the 19th and early 20th century. During these years, cowboys, many just young boys, rounded up and slowly drove millions of longhorns north from Texas to railheads in Kansas, Missouri, and Arkansas.

1861 to 1865-Civil War

The Ozarks, ravaged by both the Union and Confederate armies, were a violent and dangerous place during the four years of the Civil War. The Ozarks in southern Missouri and northern Arkansas were especially hard-hit by the war. The region was sparsely populated, making it a good haven for ex-guerrilla fighters from both sides as well as bandits and outlaws.

1865 to 1890-Outlaws and Lawmen

The years following the Civil War were a troubling time for the Ozarks. The war brought men to the area who had learned to live by the gun. Outlaws like Jesse and Frank James, as well as the Younger brothers, became folk heroes. A few men, such as James Hickok and Wyatt Earp, went on to use their guns to enforce the law.

1883 to 1889-Bald Knobbers

The Bald Knobbers, a vigilante gang, ruled the lawless post-Civil War Ozark Mountain region. The Bald Knobbers, who mostly supported the North during the American Civil War, faced opposition from the Anti-Bald Knobbers, who largely aligned with the Confederates.

Good and bad are two sides of the same coin. Sometimes good men do bad things. Sometimes bad men do good things.

Prologue

Dalton had never feared death. It was a waste of time and energy. As a preacher once warned, "No one knows when the day or hour will come, but no one escapes death."

Those words had motivated him to live every single day with one purpose: revenge. The thirst for vengeance and retribution had shaped his actions and given his life purpose. The urge to "get even" had fueled countless conflicts, from petty squabbles to death and destruction, leaving its mark on his soul.

But now, with the Grim Reaper knocking, reality set in. In the depths of his heart, he knew this was the end, but not only was he not accustomed to fear, he also did not and could not grasp it.

When the deeds of his lawless life flashed before his eyes, he realized too late that his cold heart had been a prison, one that had locked out warmth and love. He cried out for a little more time to live his life over again in a different way, but as the preacher had said years ago, "Death waits for no man."

Chapter 1

Kansas Prairie

Ma sat churning butter on the front porch. Eight-year-old Dalton could hear the soft scraping of the wooden handle as it passed up and down, up and down, turning the sweet cream into butter while he helped his pa mend the corral. Brushing back a lock of wavy blond hair, wild from hours outdoors, the thought of wild honey and butter on a hot biscuit made his mouth water.

Although he hated milking Beauty, their one and only Jersey cow, morning and night, he had to admit that it had its rewards. Milk at every meal, rich cream on wild strawberries, and hand-cranked ice cream in the winter when he'd gather enough icicles for his mother to perform this miraculous feat. Summer's mid-morning Kansas breeze was already hot, reminding him that his winter's dessert would be a long time coming.

Sweating and cursing the heat with each thud of the hammer, Pa worked. Dalton revered his father's strength and unwavering determination to complete any job he started. Young Dalton was his pa's right-hand man, fetching and helping him with anything and everything. Repairing the corral was the first of many projects his father had planned. Satisfied with the day's work, Pa celebrated by taking Dalton skinny-dipping in the creek. "We work hard, son, but we must play too!"

Ma surprised them with a scrumptious supper that evening. She had killed and plucked one of her twenty or so chickens, and it was fried and heaped up on a big platter in the center of the kitchen table. Vine-ripened tomatoes, skillet-fried taters, and a wild gooseberry cobbler topped off the end of this glorious day.

Dalton was the first to spot dust rising on the eastern horizon. Horses, moving swiftly, spelled trouble. His pa said the country was being terrorized by whiskey-drinking, foul-mouthed marauders who were trying to bring slavery into the territory. They burned out and often killed any who opposed them.

Dalton pointed and shouted, "Pa, riders!"

His father, seeing the dust clouds, pushed back his chair from the supper table and took to the front porch with Ma and Dalton close behind. He wondered aloud, "How many riders does it take to raise a storm like that one?" He guessed at least a dozen horsemen were bearing down on them.

He yelled, “Kora, get inside and bolt the door!”

The riders were getting close. Pa could hear the hoof beats now, probably within minutes of his family. He grabbed Dalton by the shoulders. “Son, run—run for the fields. Hide and don’t come out ‘til I call for you.”

“No, Pa, please let me help!” Dalton pleaded.

“Hush! Hide and be very quiet.”

Dalton escaped to the nearby stand of corn behind the cabin. From his hiding place, he watched as his father dashed for the rifle propped by the front door.

It was too late; two of the riders dismounted and trapped him at the bottom of the porch steps. One of the outlaws, tall and large-boned, with shaggy black hair and an untrimmed mustache, grabbed Dalton’s father, pinning his arms behind his back. Cursing, he struggled but could not break free. The other man, sporting a bulging belly beneath his worn shirt and stringy, unkempt dark-brown hair dangling over his sunken cheeks, forced him to his knees.

Two more men kicked open the cabin door. The first to enter grabbed Dalton's mother by the hair and dragged her down the wooden steps, screaming and kicking. His scraggly beard clung to his pointed chin, which did little to conceal uneven, yellowed teeth as he sneered. The second man, squint-eyed with a pockmarked face and a crooked nose that looked like it had been broken multiple times, forced Dalton's mother to kneel beside his father.

What Dalton witnessed next was forever seared into his mind. One, a mountain of a man with sharp blue eyes, dark hair, and beard, remained on his horse and coldly stared down at his beloved parents struggling in the dirt. “You were warned, Ean Parnell. It didn’t have to come to this,” he yelled, pulling his revolver.

Dalton’s ma was shot first. As his pa cried out, “No!” a second blast rang out. It was over in an instant.

Pointing to the cabin, the executioner ordered a short, heavy-set man with wild, fiery red hair that matched his thick, bushy beard, “Dutch, burn’er to the ground!”

The boss man never moved from his saddle as his raiders pilfered the cabin for valuables. Before riding away, they set fire to the homestead and then left in a cloud of dust just as they had arrived.

Dalton staggered from the field to his parents, wrapping his arms around their still-warm bodies and weeping. Through his tears, he noticed the silver watch chain clutched in his father’s hand. Reaching out, he tugged at it, pulling the timepiece from his father’s lifeless fingers. As he picked up the watch, it felt familiar and comforting in his hand.

He remembered standing with his father for a long time on the sidewalk, gazing at the silver pocket watch in the store window. This wasn’t the first time he had stood in that same spot, observing his father admire the timepiece and wishing for it. But on this day, Pa went inside the store and asked the clerk to show him the pocket watch up close. It would cost him a year of hard work and careful saving, but he wanted that watch. He had been putting back as much as he could for some time.

The following week, he returned and made the purchase. For a man in his position—a homesteader who worked tirelessly to provide for his family—it was a luxury. However, he was pleased to have bought it, and now, so was Dalton.

Alone, Dalton sat until dark. The raging fire reduced his home to a pile of smoldering embers. Everything he loved was gone. But now, there was a new fire stirring within him; one that would shape his destiny.

Chapter 2

Kansas Prairie

In the early morning, Thomas Harper unbolted the cabin door and stepped out. His wife, Martha, grabbed the shawl from the wall hook and followed. The air hung heavy with the scent of smoke—a bitter reminder of the violence that had swept through the prairie the night before. Kansas, still raw and untamed, knew too well the terror of marauders who left scorched ruins and broken families in their wake.

Thomas and Martha saddled their horses and rode the familiar path; the ground now blackened underfoot with splintered fences jutting out like the bones of some ancient beast. The Harpers exchanged a glance, and Thomas urged his horse faster, heart pounding with a premonition neither dared voice.

When the remains of the Parnell cabin came into view, a shudder passed through them. Charred and broken, its timbers collapsed upon themselves like a deck of folding cards. Smoke still whispered from the wreckage, curling in the morning air.

Martha was the first to see him. He sat beside the lifeless forms of his parents. She knelt beside the boy, her hand gentle on his shoulder, her voice barely above a whisper. "Oh, child," she breathed, brushing away a lock of hair from his brow.

Dalton, motionless amid the ashes, his face streaked with soot and tears, looked up with eyes wide and haunted, reflecting the ruin of his world. No words passed his lips; the horror had stolen them, leaving only silence.

Thomas lifted the boy into his arms. Dalton did not resist. His gaze remained distant, searching for meaning in a world that had collapsed into chaos. The Harpers wrapped the boy in a blanket, shielding him from the morning wind, and took him away from the place that had, just hours before, been his home.

Dalton's arrival at the Harper homestead was the beginning of a new chapter in his life. The sturdy log cabin was filled with the warmth and the kindness of his new family. Martha made sure he ate, coaxing food past his lips with patient hands. Thomas taught him how to work the land: planting, tending, and harvesting.

Dalton accepted their kindness in silence,

his gratitude buried beneath grief. Nights found him staring across the prairie, his mind replaying the horror of flames and gunshots, the cries of his parents echoing in his dreams. The Harpers gave him space, hoping time would mend the wound.

There were moments when Dalton responded—a half-smile at a joke, the careful way he learned to plow a straight furrow. But these glimmers of hope never lasted. He remained haunted by the painful memory of loss.

One evening, Martha sat at the kitchen table, her hands wrapped around a mug of coffee, concern etched across her face. "Thomas, the boy didn't say a word all day. Not even when I asked if he wanted more cobbler at dinner. He's always so still. It's been weeks now."

"I know, Martha. It's not just quiet, it's like he's somewhere else entirely. I saw him out in the yard, just staring at the fence. I tried telling him about the horses, but he looked right through me."

"Do you think we should take him to someone? Maybe the doctor in town."

"What would a doctor say? His whole world changed the night those men came." Thomas paused, then continued, "The boy saw things no child should ever have to. I can't imagine what's in his head now."

"I just wish he'd talk, Thomas. A word, anything. Sometimes I hear him whisper at night, but it's so faint I can't make it out." Sighing, she said, "I don't want to push him, but... I'm scared for him."

"Now, Martha, we have to give him time. We can't force the boy. Being here with us and attending church is all we can do for now."

And so, each Sunday morning, Dalton sat in the back of the family's wooden wagon, his legs dangling over the lowered tailgate as the wheels rolled steadily down the dusty road. He rarely noticed the beauty along their route to the white clapboard church on the hill. Instead, his eyes inevitably wandered to a scar on the landscape—a blackened patch of earth—and to the skeletal remains of a house that once echoed with laughter and warmth.

As the wagon approached the charred ruins, his small hands would tighten around the edge of the bench. The smell of smoke and the terror he felt seemed to return each time, even though he knew he was safe now.

Martha would glance back, her eyes filled with worry, while Thomas would rest a reassuring hand on his shoulder, reminding the boy that he belonged with them.

After passing the ruins, Dalton's gaze lingered for a moment before he turned his attention forward. In the peace of the church pew, the hymns and prayers provided him with a release for his grief and a path to forgiveness. However, the memories of that terrible night overshadowed any hope of Dalton letting go of the resentment and anger: all he could see were the cruel faces of the six outlaws.

The pain inside him would not subside. It thrived, growing stronger with each passing day, fueled by the memory of the men who had taken from him his family and home. He spoke little, but when he did, his words carried a cold purpose. He inquired about the men who had come at night—who they were and where they might go next.

Thomas, wary of stoking the fire in the boy's heart, answered carefully, but Dalton's resolve deepened with every tale of violence.

Chapter 3

Kansas Prairie

Dalton stood at the edge of the homestead, looking out over the tall prairie grass waving in the glow of the sun as it slowly slipped below the horizon. Voices filled with love and happiness drifted from the log cabin behind him. He was thankful, deeply thankful for the Harpers taking him in.

Eight years had passed since the marauders swept through Kansas, leaving only ashes and sorrow in their wake. Dalton, who had been a boy too young to seek revenge but old enough to feel the pain of loss, finally came to understand that some broken hearts never mend.

The Harpers were not kin by blood, but something deeper had grown over the years. Under their care, Dalton learned to build fences, drive cattle, and shoot a rifle. However, kindness and care did not fill the void left by the loss of his parents.

As time passed, Dalton's rage grew, and his purpose sharpened. The faces of the men who had shattered his home haunted his dreams. Justice, or vengeance, called him-a call that grew louder with each passing day. But justice required more than will; it required means. Dalton needed money, which meant finding work.

The Harpers could offer him shelter, but not the money he needed to track down the marauders. So, Dalton decided to head south to Texas, where herds of longhorn cattle awaited. He would join the great drive along the Chisholm Trail, earning his own keep and returning with enough money to seek out those who'd wronged him.

The next morning, Dalton packed a small satchel, the bare necessities, a spare shirt, a knife, a pouch of what little money he had saved, and his rifle.

The Harpers gathered at the gate, their faces filled with concern. Martha hugged him tightly while pressing a biscuit and a few slices of bacon wrapped in a white cloth in his hand.

Thomas clapped him on the shoulder. "Don't go looking for trouble, son. Let the Lord right the wrong done to you years ago."

Dalton nodded, his heart full of gratitude. The rising sun at his back, he mounted his horse and set out for Texas. He rode through towns with rugged wooden buildings and dusty main streets. He slept beneath a moonlit sky filled with stars and counted every mile as a step towards justice and reckoning.

Dalton found work at JA Cattle Ranch in northern Texas, where the foreman, a grizzled man named Amos Bracken, eyed him up and down before agreeing to hire him.

"Ya ever trailed longhorn before?" Bracken asked.

"Nope," Dalton replied, "but I'm a quick learner."

Bracken grunted, and Dalton joined the ranks of drovers preparing for the Chisholm Trail.

Each day was a test of endurance and patience. The cattle were wild, horns sweeping like scythes, and the men around Dalton were a mixture of drifters, dreamers, and hard cases. He learned to ride for days on end, keep the herd together, weather the sudden violence of the prairie storms, and how to handle a six-shooter.

Chapter 4

Chisholm Trail

Dalton rode into camp, greeted by Sam, a young wrangler practicing his roping skills. He climbed down, his legs stiff, his face weary, and handed the reins to the lad as he loosened the girth to remove the saddle from his trustworthy quarter horse. Dalton hoisted the saddle over his shoulder and sauntered toward the chuckwagon as Sam tied his mare to the rope line and tended to her needs.

Hired on as part of a twelve-man crew, Dalton's job was to help drive two thousand longhorns hundreds of miles over the Chisholm Trail from the south Texas grazing land north to the railhead in Abilene, Kansas. This undertaking had not been without perils. On the long trip—nearly two months—the cattlemen had forged two major rivers: the

Arkansas River and the Red River. They had endured the badlands, climbed mountains, and crossed Indian Territory. They faced rustlers and fought the weather. And they had done all of this while trying to corral a herd of contrary longhorns.

Slapping his goatskin gloves against leather chaps, Dalton headed for the campfire, where three cowhands were silently sipping coffee. *It didn't matter how rough men were,* Dalton thought, *Let death visit camp, and it puts them to thinking*.

He dropped his saddle near the men and walked to the back of the chuckwagon. He relived the hell of the stampede as he rinsed both hands and face from the small pan of water.

It had all started around midnight. The wind picked up, howling over the bare Kansas prairie, stirring up dust. With a soft creak of old leather, Dalton shifted his frame in the saddle, tugged the brim of his hat lower over his eyes, and pulled the bandana up over his mouth and nose.

As usual, the animals were jumpy and skittish before a storm. They would not bed and were restlessly moving here and there.

Back at camp, the cowpokes watched the skies. Soon, the full moon was obscured by dark grey rain clouds. “Come on, boys!” the old hand yelled to the younger men gathered around the cookfire.

He knew what was coming. He saddled up and took out across the plains toward the herd, followed by every man in camp.

Then it hit in a full fury of wind and rain. A sudden golden streak of lightning ripped open the heavens. Cattle bellowed in fear. A second bolt illuminated the plains—the terrified cattle and the riders stood out in the eerie bluish moment—and then all hell broke loose.

A rider's horse reared and shrieked with terror, throwing the man. Dalton heard the fear in the man's voice as he yelled, "Dalton, over here!"

A vengeful grin spread behind Dalton's bandanna as horns clashed, hooves pounded, and the ground shook. With a roar like an earthquake, the herd ran, trampling the downed man, drowning out the screams.

Dalton could have saved the horseless rider, but he didn't. He had recognized the cowhand the day he signed on for the cattle drive. The squinty-eyed, pockmarked face was the same that looked down cruelly on his mother while she was shot that day by the big man on horseback.

The man deserves no mercy for the wrong he did, Dalton figured, turning his attention to the stampeding cattle. He knew holding the herd was out of the question. The only thing to do was for someone to get in the lead alongside the longhorns and try to head them running in a circle before they scattered to hell and gone.

Dalton couldn't see the herd or the other riders except when a flash of lightning lit up the sky. He rode at a dead run in the dark down the retreating column to get up beside the leaders at the head of the stampede. Joined by another rider, they were able to turn the steers to the right, forming a circle.

The other men posted their locations by firing several shots at a time while keeping the herd rushing wildly round and round. They worked at tightening the circle until the cattle ran themselves out.

Several cowboys began singing to the exhausted animals. The lullaby soothed the jittery longhorns. The herd, well over its scare, was returned to its bed-ground near camp.

Cooke interrupted Dalton's thoughts. "Bacon in the pan, coffee in the pot," he said, pointing to the fire. He then filled a tin plate with beans, lifted the lid of the cast-iron Dutch oven, scooped out a hot biscuit, and handed it to Dalton.

Dalton helped himself to several slabs of meat, poured a cup of strong black coffee, and squatted with the others.

A wrangler known only as Cactus Jack said, "The way I figure it, the pace we're settin' ought to have us in Abilene by tomorrow. I don't reckon the boss would begrudge us seein' the sights."

All eyes turned on Cactus Jack in surprise. That was as many words as he had spoken since they had left Texas.

"I hear it's a wide-open town." Cooke smiled and added, "Gambling, whiskey, and fancy women!"

"How 'bout good eats?" Cody, the youngest of the men, teased Cooke.

The men continued laughing and joking about the good times to be had in Abilene. Dalton didn't join in. Stomach full, he stretched out on his blanket and watched the darkening sky. The coyotes tuned up for their evening concert, and somewhere in the distance, a cow bawled for her lost calf.

He felt the flames of vengeance licking at his soul. Today, one of the six bit the dust. No matter how long it took, he vowed to hunt down the rest of the raiders who had murdered his parents. He whispered to the night, "I will kill them all."

On the trail, life was rough and monotonous. He was in the saddle for fourteen to sixteen hours during the day and several additional hours during his night shift. Between night duty and early rising, he could never get more than a few hours of sleep. It was dirty, smelly, dangerous, and exhausting work for only $25 a month.

He had faced storms, stampedes, outlaws, Indians, and rattlesnakes. He decided, *No more driving longhorns and eating dust. Abilene is end of the trail!* Besides, the way he figured it, if Abilene was a "wide-open" cowtown as Cooke had said, the big man and the rest of his band would ride in sooner... or later, and he would be waiting.

Chapter 5

Abilene, Kansas

"We'll be travelin' 'bout daylight. If you're not here, we'll leave without ya." The trail boss's words came back to Dalton as he walked down Texas Street away from the Drovers Cottage Hotel and the Great Western Stockyards.

When the herd was sold, Dalton drew his pay. He purchased a completely new change of clothes, from tight-fitting dress boots to a new Stetson. He removed the grime of the trail, visited a barbershop, then donned his new duds and strapped on a pair of pearl-handled Colts. He had no intention of returning to Texas. He had business in this railroad cowtown.

From the moment he ambled into the Dover Cottage, dust trailing from his boots and the brim of his hat casting a shadow over his eyes, he knew he had made the right choice. The three-story wood-frame structure with about a hundred rooms had been his home for the rest of the summer and the winter. The broad veranda along the front of the hotel afforded him a perfect vantage point of the town and stockyards.

Tenants included mostly drovers and cowboys, but there was a third group calling the hotel home. They divulged very little about their past, and no one ventured to press the point. Dalton fell into this last group.

He liked Abilene. Wild and untamed, it was like no other. Half the year, it was like most of the sleepy frontier towns across Kansas. But with spring, Abilene quickly transformed into a violent and dangerous boomtown. Thousands of longhorns from Texas began to arrive, and the streets teemed with rowdy, drunken cowboys.

Dalton was betting it was a place the men he sought would be drawn to, a town drowning in greed and easy money. Stores, saloons, and gambling houses competed for the patronage of the cowboys, while the dance halls and brothel houses catered to their lust. A town where good was outmatched by evil.

For months, Dalton followed a well-thought-out routine. Most of his day was spent sitting in the lobby, and at night he frequented the saloons. By simply being present—unassuming, quiet, and watchful—he became invisible in plain sight. He learned the value of patience, the beauty of restraint, and the importance of letting others speak freely. The best way to gather what he needed was not to interrogate or intimidate, but simply to listen. Information, like the wind across the prairie, found its own way to those wise enough to wait.

Dalton eased himself into a battered leather armchair near the lobby's marble fireplace, settling his hat low enough to shade his eyes but high enough to see. Behind the check-in desk, a bored clerk thumbed through the morning paper. To his left, an older woman stood looking out the window at the falling rain.

He watched as people entered and exited—a wagon driver grumbling about a broken wheel, a pair of local cowboys arguing softly in the corner, and the hotel clerk answering questions impatient to get back to his paper. Dalton observed, never speaking, content to let the ebb and flow of conversation move around him like water around a stone.

Two men stood near the grand piano. They wore the dust of hard travel, and their posture suggested they were accustomed to danger. The pair leaned in close. The skinny fellow with a scar running from ear to chin kept his voice barely above a whisper. His companion, a burly, sharp-eyed man, watched the doorway as if expecting trouble.

"Heard they're camped just past the cottonwoods," the burly man murmured. "Not more than a mile. Kansas men. Killers, the lot of 'em." On the run since that shootout in Dodge City."

Dalton's demeanor did not change. He neither shifted in his seat nor betrayed any sign of interest. But beneath the brim of his hat, his eyes were open—watchful—and his breathing slowed to a measured rhythm. He caught every word, every hurried syllable.

"Reckon they're waitin' for dark to ride in," the thin man replied, fingers tapping a jittery rhythm on the whiskey glass. "Some say they put three in the ground just last week."

"Best to stay away from the Bull Head Saloon. Heard that was their favorite hangout," advised the other man.

The two continued their whispered plans on how they might slip out of town before trouble arrived. Finally, they stood, crossed the lobby, and left the hotel.

The world around Dalton faded. The clerk's yawn, the woman's sigh, the hiss of rain against the window, all receded into the background. The weight of his pledge to avenge his parents' deaths pressed on him like the storm that gathered beyond the hotel walls. "Tonight, it will end," he whispered.

Chapter 6

Abilene, Kansas

Dalton turned on Cedar Street, and to all who might take notice, he was just a cowboy out looking for a good time. He appeared to glance with little interest at the Alamo Saloon as he passed, yet his steel-gray eyes missed nothing. It offered a shiny mahogany bar with carefully polished brass fixtures.

From the back of the bar, a large mirror reflected the glass bottles of amber liquor. He counted a dozen customers. They looked like bankers and businessmen for the most part, not the kind of people eager to strike up a conversation with a cowboy. *A bit fancy for my taste*, he thought.

It was hard to miss the striking appearance of the man in expensive, showy attire, playing cards at one of the gaming tables that covered the entire floor. Yellow hair down to his shoulders, piercing gray eyes, and a flowing mustache made Wild Bill Hickok a figure to attract attention. *A good place to stay away from*, Dalton noted.

Hickok, the newly appointed marshal, was well-known before he came to Abilene. What added to his fame was the deadly marksmanship he displayed in keeping the town quiet and orderly.

Citizens, drunken trail hands, including Dalton, all gave him a wide berth. It was not a good idea to draw the curiosity of this lawman.

Dalton continued down Cedar Street to the Bull Head, a saloon he had frequented many times during his stay in Abilene. It was a plain-looking joint with a simple bar of pine lumber for standing drinkers.

The main room on the first floor was open to the second story. A half-dozen wooden tables and chairs were scattered around. There was a piano on one side of the room, although Bull Head didn't currently employ a piano player.

Instead of a mirror, it featured a painting of a woman lounging on a bed with nothing to hide her ample charms except for the strategically placed wisp of cloth. It was the kind of art he could appreciate.

Dalton gave it careful consideration while he sipped at his drink. The whiskey was passable, and he liked the feel of the place: the lazy undercurrent of trouble that hummed just below the surface of things.

Dalton liked the saloon. He liked the manly

smell of beer and tobacco smoke. He liked the easy smiles and flirting manner of the fancy ladies. When inclined, he went upstairs to a room with one.

Dalton lingered at the bar, waiting and watching for the men who had ridden into town at sundown. *They'll all be dead before sunrise*, he vowed.

He didn't have long to wait. Out front, riders dismounted. Tethering the horses, they tromped, spurs jingling, up onto the wooden boardwalk. Dalton turned in time to see the first through the door, a mountain of a man, with sharp blue eyes, dark hair, and beard.

Despite the heat, he still wore a long coat; every part of him, from the top of his hat to the worn boots on his feet, was covered in a fine layer of yellowish-brown dust. Dalton noticed the showy way he pushed the side of his coat back, so it caught behind his gun and holster.

The face, long ago seared into his mind, Dalton immediately recognized the leader of the raid on his family's homestead. He searched the faces of the other four dirt-caked cowboys who next stepped through the batwing doors.

The short, heavy-set man with wild, fiery red hair tumbling untamed from beneath a weathered hat, he remembered as one of the big man's Kansas henchmen. The others, he reckoned, were new recruits.

"Where can a thirsty cowpoke get a drink around here?" the big man boomed, suddenly jovial. He strutted to the bar and stationed himself to the right of Dalton. His men followed, lining up along the bar between Dalton and their leader.

The drunk standing to the left of Dalton gulped his drink, took a lingering look at the painting, and said before scurrying for the street, "You'd better get. That big man is Morgan... John Morgan. He's been causin' trouble in these here parts for quite a spell. Heard he sometimes rides with the Bald Knobbers, vigilantes terrorizing folks in the Ozarks. He's got a streak of mean in him a mile wide. He's apt to kill ya."

Dalton did not acknowledge the warning. Instead, he pulled the silver watch from his vest pocket and flipped the cover. The only thing he had left of his father's was the timepiece; he glanced at it and whispered, "Midnight... the killing hour."

Anger contorted his face. He swung around, facing the men. "Been looking for you boys," he ground out as his right hand shot down for the pearl-handled Colt. The weight of it felt good in his palm as he pulled the iron. His quick draw was lightning-fast and deadly accurate, lethal retribution for the murder of his parents.

He aimed a shot at the first outlaw in line at the bar and fired. Not having time to turn and draw, the load entered the man's back, tore through his body, and penetrated his heart. He fell face down on the bar, blood staining the wooden planks.

Without hesitating and before anyone could react to the attack, Dalton took aim at the next man in the line; the bullet blasted the back of his head. The shot passed through his skull, punctured the brain, and exited below his chin. He crumpled to the floor at the feet of John Morgan and died instantly.

The bar erupted in chaos with the loud explosions and the unexpected smacking sound of bullets hitting flesh. Amidst frightened screams and a stream of cursing, the fancy ladies and patrons all scattered. They wanted no part of the quarrel.

"Get that son-of-a-bitch!" Morgan ordered his remaining henchmen. Jerking his pistol from the holster, Morgan volleyed four shots at Dalton while taking cover behind the bar. The bullets whizzed by Dalton, missing his head as he dove for the floor and rolled behind the nearest overturned table.

The third man at the bar dropped to his knee and fired on Dalton, but missed. Dalton returned fire. The bullet struck the gunman in the chest. The wounded man tumbled backward, firing his revolver three times into the smoke-filled room. His bullets pumped into the lifeless back of the first outlaw whose body rested across the bar.

"Bam, bam, bam!" resounded as Dalton returned, firing in rapid succession, shattering glass and splintering wood. Backing from the blood-splattered saloon, walls riddled with bullet holes, and three dead men, he disappeared into the night. Marshal Hickok would be arriving soon.

The fight in the saloon had lasted but a couple of minutes. The two remaining gunmen had just been warned; they were hunted men.

Chapter 7

Kansas Prairie

The ride had been long and hot. Dalton took refuge from the sweltering heat in the shade of a cottonwood tree. He hunkered on his heels, used his hands to scoop up some water from the creek, and drank. A fish jumped in the shallow creek with a loud plop, and the horse snorted softly as it grazed along the bank.

Hearing thundering sounds of hooves in the distance made him look up. The sun dipping below the horizon cast a golden hue across the prairie. In the distance, a cloud of dust stirred.

Dalton stood. Wiping his hands on worn trousers, he gazed through the trees along the creek bank. He counted four riders galloping toward the stream. His hands moved a little closer to the pearl-handled Colts holstered on his hips.

A posse, Morgan, or something else? No matter: if the riders were looking for trouble, they had come to the right place. He wasn't one to jump to conclusions, though, and he didn't believe in running, so he stood his ground and waited for the horsemen to come to him.

Loud talk and laughter drifted over the prairie to Dalton. Their relaxed behavior suggested they might be cowboys just blowing off steam.

When the riders neared the creek, they noticed Dalton and his horse for the first time. They slowed their mounts but didn't stop, approaching the creek at a more cautious pace. The four spread out a little, signaling they had the advantage in a gunfight.

The horsemen came to a stop on the other side of the creek. Young, not much older than fifteen or sixteen, they already had a hard look about them. All carried handguns and rifles stuck up from saddle scabbards on their horses. Despite their age, they all had the look of men who knew how to use the weapons.

Dalton took note of their interest in the two guns strapped to his waist and the Winchester on his saddle as well. It was clear that, despite their youth, they knew to be wary.

One edged his horse a little ahead of the others. Brown curls spilled from under his wide-brimmed, low-crowned hat. The stubble on his cheeks marked him as the oldest and probably the leader. Pushing back the hat, he leaned forward and asked, "Mind if we water our horses, mister?"

Dalton waved his left hand toward the creek. "Help yourself. Not my water."

The young rider motioned for his band of dusty, sun-weathered boys to dismount. Dalton took note of how they did it one at a time so that somebody would always be watching him.

The leader tried to make small talk as the horses drank, asking, "Where ya from?"

When Dalton didn't answer, the kid volunteered, "We're from Texas."

"What are you doing in Kansas?" Dalton questioned, eyes alert.

"Drove a herd of cattle to the stockyards in Abilene. After weeks of eaten' dust and staring at the rear ends of hundreds of longhorns, we collected our pay and headed for the nearest saloon. The kid paused and then looked the stranger in the eye. "The Bull Head."

Dalton understood. The boy gang could identify him as the shooter at the saloon. With an icy stare, he edged aside the lapel of his white duster so the revolvers in his gun belt were revealed.

The youngest looking of the group ripped out a curse and reached for his gun. He stopped short of grabbing it when he saw that the stranger's hands were already resting on the pearl-handled Colts.

Witness to the shootout in the cowtown, the young man held up both hands and said, "Whoa, we don't want any trouble, mister. We just want to water our horses and hit the trail back to Texas."

Deadly calm, Dalton stared back at the boy

and warned, "If I were to find out that you lied, I wouldn't take kindly to it."

"You won't have any reason to look us up. I swear it," the kid promised, wiping sweat from his forehead with a dirty bandana.

"All right," Dalton agreed with a nod.

He watched the four swing up into their saddles and heeled their mounts into motion. The animals' hooves splashed in the water as the young cowpokes took out across the creek. The riders angled away from the stream so they could still see the stranger from the corner of their eyes as they rode east in a hurry.

The youngest of the group suddenly reined in his horse and headed in a hard gallop back to the creek.

Dalton reached for his Winchester and waited.

At the water's edge, the boy yelled, "Hey, mister, if you're looking to finish what you started in Abilene, I know where your friends are headed."

"Where?"

"I heard them arguing about their next move. Not sure who was after them, they finally decided their best bet was to split up. The big man, his redheaded sidekick, and several other men outside the saloon with the horses took out for Tombstone in Arizona Territory, the others headed east to Missouri."

He watched the boys disappear into the prairie. A faint smile tugged at the corner of Dalton's mouth. Young, looking for trouble, he was sure the four cowboys had no intention of making the long ride back to Texas. Swinging into the saddle, he followed their dust trail.

Chapter 8

Missouri River

At sunrise, Dalton rode up a steep bluff. He reined in on a high point and gazed out across the green valley. Below, in wisps of smoke rising from the trees, he spotted the boys' camp on the Kansas side of the Missouri River.

What are they up to? He had a hunch that the young cowboys were up to no good, whatever it was.

Dalton followed the group's movements for the rest of the morning and the first part of the afternoon. When the riders crossed the river into Missouri, he followed until evening.

Sun low in the west, Dalton watched the four make camp. He sprang down and slid his rifle from the scabbard. Crouching, he moved from tree to tree until he was only feet from the camp. Flattening, he crawled behind a brush pile and peered out.

Well hidden by a pine thicket, the boys sat in the shadows. The warm, comforting scent of burning wood and the bottle of dark-colored spirits passed around the fire calmed jittery nerves.

A skinny, wiry fellow stood and raised the bottle to the heavens. He spat at the fire and declared, "Boys, this is gonna be like shooting fish in a barrel."

The youngest danced around the fire, shouting, "Yip Yee, we're going to be outlaw legends!"

The leader scratched at the stubble along his jawline and then pushed back the wide-brimmed hat. His face was split in a wide smile, and his blue eyes danced with amusement.

As the others howled in agreement and gulped the whiskey, Dalton used the last rays of daylight to scout the heavily wooded area to get a lay of the land. Winding through the trees, he found a well-traveled road. He picked his way carefully along, dodging the permanent ruts left by the six-foot wheels of stagecoaches. Standing between ruts, he studied the road. "*Damn, the wanna-be outlaws are planning a hold-up.*"

Dalton decided to stick around to see how the plan played out, considering stagecoach companies always took steps to protect their shipments, including hiring shotgun riders. Armed with sawed-off, double-barreled shotguns, these gunmen guarded valuable cargo through lawless terrain. They were tough, fighting men who risked their lives every time they climbed into the front boot of a coach.

The next day, Dalton trailed the boys. He hid in the shadows and watched as they positioned themselves for the robbery. They chose a secluded spot near a bend in the road, where the stagecoach would be forced to slow down. The lead bandit stepped behind a large rock and signaled the others to take the horses and hide in the brush along the road.

Dalton heard the stage before it came into sight at the north end of the road. Behind the pounding heels of the four horses, the two-ton Wells Fargo stage bounced and swayed from side to side. The four passengers inside clung to their seats as the stage sped along with dust clouds billowing behind.

As the stagecoach approached the bend in the road, it slowed. The masked robbers emerged from hiding on horseback, guns drawn, blocking the path. The driver pressed his foot on the brake and called to the lead horses, reining them to a halt.

The leader leveled the Winchester at the reinsman and the gunman next to him. Never taking his eyes off the two, he ordered, "Throw down your guns."

The two grudgingly obeyed, tossing their weapons to the road.

Although the leader had not been in the business of robbing stages long, he knew one thing for sure: any Wells Fargo coach accompanied by a shotgun rider carried a strongbox filled with treasure. Eyes narrowing to slits, he demanded, "Now, hand over the strongbox!"

The driver nervously fingered the reins of his four-horse team as he stared down the yawning barrel of the highway robber's rifle. For a moment, he hesitated, then reached for the strongbox. Dragging the wooden chest from underneath his seat, he tossed it overboard.

Jumping down beside the box, the bandit looked over his shoulder at the others and yelled, "If they dare to move, shoot to kill, boys!"

Looking around, the driver saw three rifle barrels aimed directly at his stage. The driver was sure that a large outlaw gang was holding him up. He had no way of knowing that he was about to become the first victim of the wanna-be stagecoach robbers.

The leader grabbed the strongbox and shook it in the air. The jingle of coins from within brought a chorus of yelps from the three other horsemen.

With a smile, he strapped the box to his saddle while a second masked man demanded of the driver, "Throw me the mailbag." Catching it with one hand, he hung it over the saddle horn.

A third masked man waved his six-shooter at the stage and demanded, "Everyone on the ground."

The passengers, driver, and guard obeyed. Once lined up in front of the coach, the robber demanded. "Now, empty your pockets."

The driver stepped forward and started to protest, but was stopped by the gun pointed at his chest. Stepping back in line, he shook his head at the shotgun rider not to interfere. The three men and the woman passengers obeyed in silence.

The masked bandit gathered the money and jewelry, stuffing what was handed over into his pockets. Once the valuables were secured, the outlaws mounted their horses. Whooping and hollering, they lit out for the woods.

Underestimating the real danger involved, the boys made one fatal mistake. They took their eyes off the shotgun rider. Wells Fargo hired gunmen for their skill with firearms and willingness to fight if attacked by bandits.

Grabbing his shotgun from the ground, he was able to get off two rounds at the backs of the fleeing robbers while the passengers quickly piled into the coach. Once the doors slammed shut, the driver whipped the horses to a gallop and put as much distance between the stage and the bend in the road as possible.

Dalton followed the young outlaws into the thicket. Tracking them turned out to be an easier job than expected. It wasn't long before he discovered a trail of blood and a blood-stained mailbag cut open. Leaning from the saddle, he latched onto the bag and looked inside for registered letters, which often held paper money or gold dust. *Empty*!

He continued through the woods and soon came upon a trail of silver dollars dropped as the fugitives fled. A quarter of a mile further along the path, Dalton found the dead boys.

One, the skinny, wiry fellow, was hunched over in his saddle, blood dripping from his chest. The other, the scruffy-faced leader, lay where he had fallen, with money and jewelry scattered in the brush. The shattered strong box, now empty, lay near the bodies.

What was left of the band of boy outlaws had vanished. Young and inexperienced, they had not taken into account that stagecoach robbery was a risky business and retribution swift.

Those who tried were usually caught and hanged or killed within a few days. Had these young outlaws approached their "work" more cautiously, they might have avoided or at least postponed their day of reckoning.

Dalton took a few minutes to gather the money. The generous donation was a welcome surprise. He would need a few extra dollars where he was headed... Arizona Territory.

Chapter 9

Santa Fe Trail

There was no sound but the footfalls of Dalton's horse and the creak of the saddle leather as he rode along the Santa Fe Trail. The marauders were fleeing west, unaware that vengeance was riding their back trail and drawing closer.

Sweat stung Dalton's eyes as his gaze searched the vast Kansas grasslands that stretched out in all directions. Nothing moved, silent for the rustle of the long grass in the wind. Then the earth trembled. On the horizon appeared a vast, dark mass of buffalo. Thicker than stars in the night sky, the buffalo herd extended the whole length of his afternoon ride, not in hundreds, but he reckoned in the thousands.

The sun was dropping in the sky, and long

blue shadows were being painted on the flatland around him. Despite the extreme heat and lack of fresh water, Dalton was able to cover 15 to 20 miles a day, entering the New Mexico Territory before sunset, six weeks after the stagecoach robbery in Missouri.

Hearing the beat of hooves, Dalton slid his Winchester from the scabbard and swung out of the saddle. He scrambled up the steep side of the mesa and looked out across the flat-topped hill to the featureless plains stretched out below.

A horseman was riding with his spurs flying, a ribbon of dust streaming behind him. A band of bare-chested Kiowa followed. Guiding their horses with their knees, the warriors launched a swarm of arrows.

The horseman, outnumbered by warriors feared for their brutal tactics, was a dead man running. No one could save him now.

Dalton watched one Kiowa maneuver his horse alongside the fleeing horseman. Pulling closer, the warrior knocked the man's hat off, grabbed his red hair, and pulled the man from his horse.

The Kiowa held the heavy-set, bearded man close beside his racing horse. The man's feet thrashed in a crazy dance. The dark-skinned man clutched the horseman powerfully by the hair as he scalped the man without slowing his horse, dragging his body so that dust arose in their wake.

Then, with a contemptuous movement, the warrior's last knifing slash split the man's gullet from ear to ear. The warrior flung the dead body aside. He held aloft a fiery tuft of hair and let out a yell that carried over the prairie as clear as the wail of a coyote at night.

Dalton mentally crossed off another marauder from his list. He felt nothing, no joy or sorrow, for the way the man came to his end. Death was part of life; the outlaw had chosen. It awaited the good, the bad, and anything that walked, crawled, or drew breath.

He knew the Reaper would be calling one day, maybe one day soon, for there was no denying that the path of revenge and retribution he had chosen was dangerous and deadly.

Dalton hesitated, took one last look at the man on the ground, then turned, climbed down the hill, and stepped into the saddle. He swung the horse to the south and lit out in a gallop.

Chapter 10

New Mexico Territory

Dalton reached inside the canvas duster and found his father's watch. "Almost ten until noon," he mumbled. Snapping the cover shut, he continued following the parallel ruts leading across the endless prairie.

Later in the afternoon, a lone Conestoga came into sight. A man, surrounded by a woman and two young boys, was struggling to lift the wagon to replace one of its back wheels.

One of the boys alerted his father to the lone rider approaching. Reaching for his rifle, the man stepped in front of his family.

Reining in his horse, Dalton smiled and said, "Looks like you could use another hand."

Looking the rider over, the man finally nodded and answered, "We sure could, mister."

Dalton dismounted, took off his duster, and

threw it across the saddle. Turning, he noticed all eyes were focused on the two Colts at his hips. Picking up the wooden pole discarded by the blond-headed boys when he approached, Dalton shoved it under the wagon next to the axle. Motioning for the boys to help push down on the pole, they lifted the wagon.

Working quickly, the father removed the damaged wheel, guided the new wheel onto the axle, and tightened the nut. At the father's signal, Dalton and his helpers lowered the wagon.

The boys whooped and hollered as the man shook hands with the family's rescuer. "Thanks, mister."

"Dalton Parnell, sir," he replied.

Shaking hands, the man said, "Roy Conrad, and this is my wife, Opal."

Dalton tipped his hat. "Ma'am."

Opal pointed to her sons. "This is our youngest, Willie, and J.B., our oldest.

Dalton nodded. "Boys."

"If lucky, we can catch up with the wagon train before nightfall. Join us," Roy invited.

Agreeing, Dalton helped Roy hitch the horses to the wagon while the rest of the family loaded the tools used to repair the wheel into the back.

Dalton rode along behind the family of four as they rolled and bumped their way southward across the New Mexico prairie. The sun was setting in the west when the wagon train camp came into sight.

Greeted by the wagon master, Arron Colley,

and armed guards, the Conrad wagon joined the circle of prairie schooners. Roy introduced Dalton and explained the assistance he had given with the wheel while the boys unhitched the team; Opal then started preparing supper.

Colley eyed the rider, quick to notice the Winchester and Colts. His biggest problem was the shortage of guards, so he said, “Welcome, we could use a man like you.”

Dalton joined the wagon train. He reckoned it was safer than trying to outrun a band of Kiowa. Besides arriving in Tombstone as a member of a wagon train, he would just be another pioneer looking for a chance at a new life.

Assigned to help the Conrad family, he soon adapted to the wagon train’s routine. Each day began the same. Awakened before dawn by Roy’s burley voice

“The days a wastin, there’s chores to be done before we hit the trail.”

Opal would kindle the morning fire and then prepare coffee and breakfast. After breakfast, she cleaned the dishes and repacked the wagon.

Dalton and the boys spread out to gather the grazing cattle and horses.

Roy hitched the team and pulled the wagon out of the circle into the caravan.

“Wagons Ho!” the wagon master would cry, and another day began on the Santa Fe Trail. Dozens of covered wagons hit the dusty path as brave pioneers continued their journey west.

After five or six hours of travel, the wagon

master would look for a noonday resting place. Roy would pull the wagon to a stop, unhitch the horses, and let them rest and graze. The family and Daltan would gather to eat a cold lunch, often leftovers from supper the night before. Then, the train would rest for an hour or so before prodding on.

Along the trail, Opal and the boys would look for wood to gather. Dalton and other hunters searched for game for supper.

The wagon master kept his eye out for a suitable evening campsite. A place with water, firewood, and forage for the livestock.

As the sun became lower in the western sky, the lead wagon would circle, followed by the others. The prairie schooners rolled into position, and the animals were unhitched. The wagon tongue and chains were used to connect each into a corral. Fuel wood was gathered, and campfires started. Guards were selected, and the livestock set loose to graze.

Again, it was time for the evening meal, mending clothes, repairing wheels, washing dishes, and resting. Sometimes, Roy and Dalton would gather with the other men to smoke, visit, and play cards. Each night, one old fellow would pull out his fiddle.

Dalton enjoyed hearing the sing-alongs and watching the dancing. He couldn't help smiling as the young men and women grew acquainted while dancing, which often led to countless stolen kisses in the shadows where parents could not see or hear the whispered sweet words.

Weary after a day of traveling 15 or 20 miles, the pioneers soon settled down; music faded away, the campfires dwindled, and the encampment slept.

On the fifth day, the wagons made camp for the night along a small but clean-flowing creek. Dalton helped move the livestock downstream to keep the water upstream clean for drinking and cooking. He looked south along the trail. "Damn!" he declared as the dust cloud bellowed toward the corralled wagons.

Dalton raced back to the wagon train. "Get in the wagons!" he yelled at the pioneers. Reaching the Conrads, he repeated his order to Opal and the boys as the cloudy onslaught closed in.

Turning to Roy, he demanded, "Listen carefully. You take your shotgun. Go to the front wheel. Do not fire till they come around your side and you gotta clear shot at their back."

Dalton stood behind the back wheel and watched the approach of the bandits. The oncoming riders opened fire as soon as they were within range. Forming two groups, they surrounded the wagons.

Dalton counted to twelve. He aimed at the horse of the first rider, a large man with a bulging belly beneath his worn shirt and a duster flapping behind him. Stringy, unkempt dark-brown hair dangled over his sunken cheeks as he rode straight toward the wagons. Dalton fired.

The horse dropped, throwing the rider to the

ground. His next shot ended the bandit's thrashing. He had not forgotten the face of the man who forced his father to the ground before he was murdered.

Amidst the cries and neighs, the wagon train guards fired at the riders. One man took a bullet in the chest and dropped from the saddle.

Dalton immediately stepped from along his side of the wagon. He heard the hoofbeats of a rider, coming hard and fast. Dropping his Winchester, Dalton drew his Colts and fired as he turned, downing the rider.

Under a volley of fire, losing men left and right, the leader, whom Dalton recognized as John Morgan, reined in his horse. He signaled to what was left of his band of raiders to abandon the attack. Turning north, they rode across the prairie in a cloud of dust just as they had arrived.

Except for the surviving horses and the moans of the wounded, the Santa Fe Trail was once again still and silent. Reeling from the attack, the wagon master called for a day of rest.

He instructed Dalton and the train guards to conduct a headcount to ensure no one was missing and to identify any casualties. At the same time, he went from wagon to wagon to determine what had been stolen or destroyed.

The next day, at morning's first light, Dalton swung into the saddle while Conrad tried to convince him to stay with the train and continue with them to Santa Fe. "There's safety in numbers. Out on the plains, you will be on your own."

Unable to sway his young friend, Roy finally wished him well. As Dalton turned his horse to leave, Roy said, "If you're ever back in Missouri, look up my brother-in-law, Simon Woodlee, but his men call him Boss. He owns a big cattle ranch south of Springfield. He is always looking for men who carry a gun and are not afraid to use it."

Dalton galloped across the prairie, leaving behind the family he had grown to care for, and headed toward the Arizona Territory. He was convinced that Morgan and his remaining Kansas henchmen were making their way there, and he would stop at nothing until he settled the score with blood and bullets.

Chapter 11

Tombstone, Arizona Territory

Dalton found following John Morgan and his band of raiders wasn't that difficult. Despite the better part of two days passing since the wagon attack, the tracks left by an estimated dozen mounted men were etched into the prairie. He guessed they had no cause to believe they'd be pursued, or maybe the outlaws were just so all-fired arrogant they didn't give a damn.

At nightfall, Dalton spotted the lights just beyond a flat-topped hill. A short while later, he came upon a fenced graveyard; the sign read 'Boothill.'

He knew enough about Tombstone to know it was a wild, deadly shoot-em-up town. It had sprung up around a silver mine, and with that came the outlaws, bandits, gamblers, and gunslingers. It was a good guess that many of the town's inhabitants died during violent fights, shootouts, or robberies.

He entered Tombstone at a slow pace, scanning the street. The booming mining town was lined with shops, dance halls, gambling houses, and saloons. To his left stood the Crystal Palace Saloon with a dry goods store next door. There was a narrow walkway between the two. To his right was a newspaper office and a bank.

Dalton tied up his horse outside the Crystal Palace, leaving slack enough for the bay to reach the water trough, sitting below the hitching rail. He rubbed its neck while looking at the other horses tied along each side of the street. He reckoned the bandits had corralled their horses at the livery.

Dalton mounted the wooden sidewalk, stepping to the barroom's batwing doors. Before shouldering his way through, he looked around inside.

Early yet, the bar was only half full. Several shifty-looking fellows played cards near one corner of the room. Dusty skin and clothes told the story of down-on-their-luck cowboys, looking for a quick win. Several warn-out miners stood at the bar, gray hair showing beneath felt hats, pulled down to shade their weary faces.

Dalton stepped through the doors and walked between tables to the bar. Leaving two or three arm's length between himself and the older fellows nursing beers, he motioned for the barkeep.

The six-foot, barrel-chested man approached, putting on a smile that did not reach his eyes, and said, “Gotta hand over your gun, mister. The Earps have issued a new law. No firearms within city limits. You can pick them up when ya leave.”

Dalton looked around the bar. Sure enough, no guns. Not liking the idea, he reluctantly unbuckled his holster and handed it over.

Placing the pair of Colts on a shelf under the bar, the barkeep asked, “Whiskey or beer?”

“Whiskey.”

The barkeep poured the shot. “In town for long?”

“Just passing through,” Dalton answered while looking around. The place was large enough to host a few dozen men, but he had no idea about the second story, how many scarlet ladies were in residence, or whether they had customers lined up waiting to take a turn.

He heard a door on the second story open, and he looked up in time to catch an attractive dark-haired woman stepping out. Hips swaying with each step, she made her way down the stairs and to the bar.

The ruffled bodice drew Dalton's attention to the low-cut neckline as the woman slid closer. She smiled and asked, “Buy me a drink, stranger?”

Dalton and the woman had a couple of drinks before heading upstairs to get to know each other better. He grabbed the whisky bottle, taking one last look around before climbing the stairs. The bar was beginning to fill with cowhands, miners, and locals, but he didn't see the men he was hunting.

It didn't take the woman long to shed her garments and climb into bed once their talk of business was concluded. Dalton, hearing bedsprings creaking in the next room, dug in his pocket for some coins, tossed them on the nightstand, and crawled in beside the warm body waiting for him.

Several hours later, the sound of a heated argument downstairs interrupted his evening. From one of the rooms, a woman whimpered, cut off by a man's voice telling her to shut up. Up and down the hall, he heard men scrambling to get dressed in case a fight broke out.

A fuming string of curses poured from Dalton as he scrambled around the room, pulling on his trousers and boots. He reached for his pistol belt before remembering the barkeep had it.

Furious, he cleared the doorway. Staying in the shadows, he scanned the scene below. The bar was now full of rough-looking men. He doubled back to the room.

Dalton caught a handful of the woman's tangled hair in one hand and hauled her naked out of bed. Throwing a blanket over her shoulders, he grabbed an arm and dragged her to the door.

"Let's take a walk, darling, and see what's going on downstairs," he insisted, easing along the narrow hallway to the stairs, and stopped.

Pulling free, she rubbed her arm and said, "It's men from a local gang known as the

Cowboys. Best not get involved. They're a rowdy bunch; there might be a scuffle. Don't worry; the bouncer usually settles most problems with just a glare and rarely has to knock anybody out. Nobody wants to get the law involved and have Wyatt Earp... and brothers come a calling."

Dalton eyed the table where an argument was swiftly heating up. One of the players jumped to his feet and began shouting at another.

"Whoa, now," pleaded the other.

The angry gambler reached across the table and grabbed the man by the collar. The other card players at the table jumped up and backed away.

Dalton started down the stairs. The woman caught his arm. Shaking her head, she warned, "Not a good idea," half-sounding like she gave a damn about him. She pointed to a man with a mustache and goatee, seated at a solitary corner table, cutting up a blood-rare steak. "That's the leader of the Cowboys, Ike Clanton, and every man in here is part of his outlaw gang.

Dalton watched the barkeep. Billy club dangling from his hip, he pulled a shotgun out from hiding. Before he could fire off a round, Ike Clanton stood. His scowl signaled annoyance, and his broad silhouette demanded attention.

He slammed a fist on the table, silencing the murmurs and arguments that echoed through the smoky room. He swept a cold gaze across the men, meeting each pair of eyes with his own steely resolve. "Simmer down now, boys." The boss man had spoken, and no one dared defy the order.

Out in the middle of the room, four men continued their game of poker. One, a mountain of a man with dark hair and a beard, eyed his hand, drummed a finger on the tabletop, waiting for his next card... Morgan.

Dalton was tempted but knew this was not the time or place to pick a fight with the outlaw. He needed to find out more about this cowboy gang, and then there were the Earps. It was never a good idea to draw the attention of lawmen like those three brothers.

Chapter 12

Tombstone, Arizona Territory

Dalton sat outside the Oriental Saloon, enjoying the morning sun. The Oriental was different from the other saloons in town, where cowboys would burst through the doors, dust off their clothes, down shots of cheap whiskey, and engage in brawls, breaking cheap wooden chairs over each other's heads while the bartender ducked for cover.

In contrast, the Oriental was a high-class establishment featuring ornate chandeliers, a carved mahogany bar, thick oriental carpets, and a wide selection of imported beverages served by bartenders in white coats. Every night, well-dressed patrons frequented the place, ordering from a menu that was considered one of the finest in town while enjoying music performed by skilled piano and violin players. The town's high rollers gathered in the plush gambling room, which was often visited by Wyatt Earp, who owned a share of the gaming tables.

Dalton leaned back in the wooden chair, propping his feet on the railing. He had been in town for just over a week. He was lucky to have found a room in the boomtown at the Fly's Boarding House and a stall for his horse at the nearby O.K. Corral.

He dug in the pocket of his white duster, pulling out a worn cotton tobacco pouch and a slender packet of rolling papers. With deft movements, he removed a sheet of paper and filled it with fragrant reddish-brown tobacco. He clamped the pouch between his teeth to free his other hand and, with practiced ease, rolled a cigarette.

Striking a match against the sole of his boot, he ignited the flame, which illuminated his focused expression as he lit the cigarette and tossed the match casually into the street. Taking a deep, satisfying draw, he replaced the pouch and papers while scanning the bustling scene around him. His gaze skimmed over the displays in the storefronts and the menus posted outside hotels and restaurants as he hoped to spot the men he was searching for.

He was surprised by how beneficial it was to sit quietly each day and observe. He realized he had learned much more about the town and its people this way than he ever would have by asking questions.

Tombstone, a rich mining town, attracted its

fair share of drifters, dancehall girls, outlaws, saloonkeepers, and gamblers. Respectable citizens often avoided entire sections of the town. Gunfights were common, and the unfortunate souls who fell victim to violence were quickly buried at Boothill.

Eventually, several old-timers that Dalton had gotten to know claimed the remaining chairs on the boardwalk. With nothing better to do, they gathered each morning to engage in casual conversation, tell jokes, and gossip.

The first man lit his pipe and warned, “Troubles comin’.”

A second man, whom Dalton had come to know as Tommie Long, took out a knife and a wooden stick and started whittling. “What makes you say that, Walter?”

“Some people are say’n the Earp brothers are using their badges to rise above the law, not defend it.”

A third man, a newcomer to the group, scratched his shaggy white beard and took a chew of tobacco. With his mouth full, he argued, “Ya, but others say the Earps are doing what they have to do to carry out their duties as best they can.”

Walter took a puff from his pipe. “The Earps are seen as standing in the way of ranchers like Ike Clanton and his family from doin’ business...”

The old whittler closed his knife, shoved it into the pocket of his overalls, and angrily corrected his friend, “Which includes robbing stages and rustling cattle!”

Dalton stopped the back-and-forth between the two old-timers. “Doesn’t seem to be any different than any other frontier town, to me.”

The newcomer responded, “People are willing to turn a blind eye if the Clantons’ rustling is taking place across the border in Mexico. But now, Ike is stealing from his neighbors, which is a recipe for trouble.”

Walter tried to explain, “Businessmen want Tombstone to be a respectable place where children can be raised, educated, and attend church with their families. To get a handle on the troublemakers, town leaders turned to men who had a reputation as gunfighters and lawmen.

“When the Earp brothers arrived in Tombstone, James established a saloon on Allen Street. Virgil became the deputy marshal of the town, and Wyatt and the youngest Earp went to work as lawmen, occasionally assisting their brother.”

The newcomer added, “The first day on the job, Virgil vowed to put an end to the rustling and robbing.”

Tommie took out his knife and slashed angrily at the wooden stick, sending shavings flying. “And things have gone from bad to worse! Now, Tombstone is in the center of a feud, pitting Ike Clanton and his cowboy gang against the Earps.”

“How so?” Dalton asked.

The newcomer defended Ike. “Angered by the threat of a crackdown on his business, Ike dealt with the problem. As most ranchers do when needin' help, he hired more cowboys."

"Yeah, but the difference is the men welcomed at the Clanton spread are robbers, outlaws, and rustlers looking to make money the easy way!" declared the old whittler, looking up at the newcomer and shaking his knife.

Walter added, "And word around town is that Ike has hired several men just this week who have been involved in stealing cattle from wagon trains traveling the Santa Fe Trail."

Dalton was not surprised by the information. He had suspected that Morgan and his two remaining sidekicks were working for the outlaw rancher.

Walter pounded the pipe on his hand and repacked the bowl with tobacco. Eyeing Wyatt and Doc Holiday in a deep conversation in front of the newspaper office, he declared, "It's gettin' harder and harder to tell who the bad guys are and who the good guys are in Tombstone anymore!"

"Sometimes men are both at different times," Dalton said. Flipping what was left of his cigarette to the dirt-packed street, he headed back to the boarding house.

Chapter 13

Tombstone, Arizona Territory

Dalton stood at the long mahogany bar of the Oriental Saloon. When the bartender placed a bottle and a glass in front of him, he paid with a few of the coins he had found scattered in the grass after the boy bandits' bungled stagecoach robbery.

As he finished the first drink, Dalton took a slow glance around the room. The saloon was alive with activity—piano music played in the background, conversations rang out loudly, and the smell of whiskey mingled with the sound of clinking glasses. This blend of excitement and potential danger perfectly captured Tombstone's reputation as a lawless frontier town.

His gaze was drawn to the batwing doors as Ike Clanton stumbled into the Oriental and joined a poker game. The odd part was that one of the players at the table was Virgil Earp.

Taking the bottle and glass, Dalton sat at an empty table and watched. The four gamblers focused on the poker game, intently studying their hands and placing bets. As the game went on through the night, Ike drank more and had plenty to say about Doc Holliday, none of it flattering.

Ike still held a grudge against Holliday, a friend of the Earps. The two had a heated argument at the Crystal Palace Saloon, which required Virgil to step in and separate them.

Hours passed, bets increased, and gamblers were eliminated. Eventually, only two key players remained at the table: Ike and Virgil.

They studied the last hand of the night intently. Ike fumbled with the corners of his cards. After taking a sip of his drink, he tapped his cigar on the table, sending ashes scattering over the pile of money in the center. Meanwhile, Virgil leaned back slightly, caressing his chips as he observed Ike.

Finally, Ike smirked and fanned his cards across the table, displaying three jacks. In response, Virgil said, "I have a full house, aces and sixes," then laid his hand face up on the table.

Ike jumped up, sending the wooden chair across the room. "Take the damn pot, but this is not the end! And your friend Holliday, that son-of-a-bitch is going to get what's coming to him!"

Virgil gathered the bills into a neat stack and

tucked them into his coat pocket. He smiled, dismissing Ike's threats. Ike Clanton was not known for his bravery or his desire to engage in a fight. Virgil responded, "I don't want you causing any trouble tonight and disturbing me while I'm in bed."

After a long night of watching Ike and Virgil at the poker table, Dalton was not surprised that the game ended with harsh words and threats from both sides. It was clear that tensions between the Cowboys and Tombstone's lawmen were escalating toward a showdown.

Dalton made his way back to the boarding house. The ongoing conflict between Ike, the Cowboys, and the Earps was not his concern. He had a singular purpose for being in Tombstone: to find and kill Morgan, along with any members of his gang who had allied with the Clantons.

Dalton was aware that the men he was hunting were staying at the Clanton ranch. He planned to ambush them to exact his long-awaited revenge. However, he needed to carry out his plan in a way that wouldn't attract the attention of the Earps, who were relentless lawmen willing to operate outside the law to achieve justice.

CHAPTER 14

Tombstone, Arizona Territory

Dalton found his old friends, Walter and Tommy, in their usual spot outside the Oriental Saloon.

"There's goin' a be trouble between the Clanton tribe and the Earps today," Walter proclaimed as Dalton settled in an empty chair.

Walter had been predicting a showdown between the law and the Cowboys for days. Curious, Dalton sat back and waited for the story to unfold.

Tommy paused whittling on the piece of wood that was taking the shape of a pony and said, "Bound to happen sooner or later. Tombstone is a wild town with a population of six thousand, where five thousand are bad, and one thousand are known outlaws."

"What about the Earps?" Dalton asked.

Walter puffed on his pipe for a few moments before answering, “Virgil and his brothers are tough men with questionable dealings. Some in Tombstone believe they are a gang of legalized outlaws. Others believe they are just what is needed to tame the town—good guys who are not **really** good guys.”

Tommy resumed his whittling, adding the finishing touches to the wooden toy. “Today, the Earps are the good guys.”

Walter jumped in. “It's like this, kid; sometimes good guys have to do bad things to make the bad guys pay. And this is that time! Townspeople are fed up with Ike and his gang of cattle rustlers.”

Tommy repeated what he had overheard outside The Tombstone Epitaph office earlier. “The talk in town is that a long night of poker ended in an exchange of words between Ike and Virgil. The lawman warned Ike not to cause any trouble and then went home to bed. However, too drunk to heed Virgil’s warning, having no place to stay, Ike made his way to the O.K. Corral, where he had left his horse and checked his guns.”

“On my way here, I passed him wandering the streets with a pistol and Winchester rifle, ranting and raving about the Earps and Doc Holliday,” Walter reported.

Tommy said, “When I came into town this morning, I saw Ike at the corral talking to his brother Billy, and Frank and Tom McLaury.”

Dalton and the two old-timers sat in silence, watching and waiting for what was sure to come, a showdown between the Earps and the Clantons. They did not have to wait long.

Businessmen and concerned citizens flocked to the sheriff's office until late in the afternoon. They loudly demanded that something be done about Ike.

When the Earps and Doc Holiday arrived outside the sheriff's office, they confronted the angry crowd. Finally convincing them to go home, the lawmen stormed across the street. It was clear Virgil had decided to disarm Ike and members of his gang, who had now gathered at the O.K. Corral.

The four men marched down Fourth Street. Wyatt was on the left, and to his right were Virgil, the youngest Earp brother, and Holiday. Each lawman packed a six-shooter, and Doc carried a shotgun hidden beneath his long coat.

Dalton jumped from his chair. Walter grabbed his arm. “For God's sake,” he implored, “don't follow them or you might get gunned down.”

Breaking free, Dalton said, “Don't worry, old man. I can take care of myself.”

As the four-armed men reached Fremont Street, they turned the corner with Dalton not far behind.

The lawmen entered the narrow passageway between the Harwood House and Fly's Boarding House, confronting their rivals face-to-face. Less than six feet away, Ike, Billy Clanton, Frank McLaury, his brother Tom, and two other men of the Cowboy gang stood in the lot next to the corral.

Dalton paused and stepped back into the shadows of the passageway, noticing three men inside the corral—Morgan and his two sidekicks.

When Virgil called out, “Boys, throw up your hands; I've come to disarm you,” Dalton saw the men inside the corral quickly duck down behind one of the horse stalls.

Dalton’s attention returned to the Cowboys and the Earps when Billy Clanton yelled, “Don't shoot! I don't want to fight!”

Wyatt Earp replied, “You sons-a-bitches have been looking for a fight, and now you have it.”

Before Wyatt could finish his sentence, the bullets started flying. The crack of pistols and the boom of Doc’s Winchester left Dalton's ears ringing.

Within seconds, nearly thirty shots rang out. Then, just as suddenly, silence descended on the vacant lot. The shootout was over. All that remained was the acid smell of gun smoke.

It all happened so quickly that Dalton struggled to keep track of the gunfire. From what he could tell, Billy Clanton had shot the youngest Earp through the leg and Virgil Earp through the shoulder. Doc Holliday had taken a bullet to the hip. Ike Clanton, who was unarmed, ran away as the fight began.

The remaining three Cowboys, Frank and Tom McLaury, along with Billy Clanton, lay dead on the ground. Only Wyatt was unharmed.

The sheriff, followed by a crowd of curious

townsfolk and businessmen, quickly gathered at the corral to see who had survived the gunfight. During the chaos, Dalton watched Morgan and his men ride out of the corral.

There was nothing he could do to stop them. They had escaped again, but their time was coming. In the end, the wrongdoers would get what was coming to them.

The coroner showed up first and loaded the bodies of Billy Clanton, Frank McLaury, and Tom McLaury into a wagon. Virgil, the youngest Earp brother, and Doc were carried home for treatment. Nothing left to see, the onlookers slowly began to clear out of the lot.

Dalton stepped from the shadows of the narrow passageway between the Harwood and Fly's Boarding Houses and headed to the corral. He found a young stable hand with a pitchfork scooping hay and manure from one of the stalls. It was easy to get the boy to talk about what he had seen and heard.

When asked about the three men who had taken cover in the stable, the youngster shook his head and said he didn’t know their names. After a few more questions, Dalton learned that the boy had overheard the men talking before they saddled up and tore out of the stable as if the devil were hot on their trail.

From what the kid gathered, the men feared the Earps would come after them due to their association with the Cowboys. After a brief discussion, the men agreed it might be healthier for them if they headed back east to Missouri.

Chapter 15

Arizona Territory

Dust swirled in lazy circles in front of the O.K. Corral. Dalton stood among the clatter of spurs and snorts of restless horses. The transaction was simple: a handshake with the stable owner, a last pat on the horse's neck, and the quiet exchange of silver coins.

Stuffing the money in the pocket of his white duster, Dalton strode through the shadows of the narrow passageway between the boarding houses to Fourth Street. His destination was the Wells Fargo office, its red-lettered sign swinging in the Arizona breeze. Inside, the clerk greeted him with a nod. Dalton laid his coins on the worn counter, purchasing a single ticket eastward on the stagecoach.

He stepped outside, ticket in hand, and paused. He stood apart from the others, hat pulled low over his forehead. His shirt, once blue, had faded, and the cuffs were frayed, stained with the sweat of hard travel. A pair of leather gloves hung from his belt. The Colts strapped to his waist—suggested he was no stranger to trouble.

The shootout at the corral faded behind him. His only thoughts were of getting back to Missouri.

Beside Dalton stood a preacher. He wore a black frock coat, with a starched white collar, and a silver cross hanging from a chain. His face was pale, and his hair grayed at the temples. He kept a well-thumbed Bible tucked beneath his arm.

A gambler, leading the way with a silver-tipped cane and a grin that seemed permanently stitched to his lips, approached and stood behind the preacher. His suit, black as midnight and tailored with care, caught the light with every movement, and his fingers sparkled with rings of gold. At his side clung his woman, dressed in scarlet velvet, hair piled high.

Dalton had run into the gambler at the Oriental Saloon. Known as Lucky Jacks, a fixture at the card tables, he was infamous for the way he could charm coins from a miner. There were stories that he had cheated death in Dodge and once even bluffed his way out of jail.

As they waited for the stage, Jacks produced a deck of cards and began to shuffle. He challenged Dalton to a friendly hand, but the offer was met with a stern shake of the head.

The preacher declined as well, quoting Proverbs with a gentle smile.

The stagecoach rumbled into view, its red paint dulled by dust and sun, harnesses creaking on the backs of four restless bays. The driver—a hard-looking man with a pistol at his hip and a hat as round as a frying pan—called out names from the manifest, his voice crisp and commanding.

Dalton stepped forward first, tossing his saddlebag into the luggage rack, and climbed into the coach. The preacher followed. The gambler waited until last, the woman climbing up with practiced grace.

Inside the coach, Dalton took the seat nearest the door, eyes fixed on the horizon. The preacher settled beside him, Bible open, and began a low conversation about forgiveness and hope on the road ahead. Lucky Jacks and his companion sat on the bench across from Dalton and the preacher.

As the coach lurched forward, the dusty streets of Tombstone began to slip away, replaced by the endless sweep of sage and sand, mesas rising in the distance. The sun climbed higher, and the stagecoach rolled on. In the afternoon, the waylay station emerged on the horizon.

The driver, tightening the reins, called out a greeting to the stable hands halting the stagecoach in front of the porch. The stable crew sprang into action. They approached the coach with practiced ease, soothing the fatigued horses after miles of hard travel.

The four passengers descended from the stagecoach while the driver exchanged a few words with the station's proprietor, a broad-shouldered figure whose apron bore the faint scent of flour and roast meat.

Inside, the staff moved quickly among the tables, serving steaming plates and pouring cider into tin mugs. Passengers gathered around the tables. As the meal wound down, Dalton stretched his legs along the edge of the property, searching the horizon for any sign of trouble.

Soon, the driver called out for the passengers to gather outside. The preacher finished his mug, tucking a crust of bread into his pocket for the road. The gambler and his companion exchanged warm farewells with the proprietor, gathered their belongings, and prepared to board.

Outside, the fresh team stamped their hooves impatiently, ready to hit the trail. The coach was hitched and inspected, every buckle and strap secure. The impatient driver called out, "Let's go!" The four passengers climbed aboard, settling into their seats.

The driver took his place and gave a nod to the stablemaster, who tipped his hat in return. With a sharp call and a crack of the whip, the stagecoach rolled out of the waylay station, wheels creaking in rhythm with the horses' pounding hooves.

The preacher, taking the measure of the other passengers, broke the silence first with his gentle yet firm voice, the tone of many sermons echoing beneath his words. “I’ve seen the ruin vengeance can bring,” he began, eyes fixed on the horizon. “I’ve buried good people who let anger shape their lives. There’s no peace in revenge, only a shadow that grows until it wraps the soul in darkness.”

Dalton shrugged. “Easy to say, reverend, when your life’s been about forgiveness.”

The preacher’s eyes darted to Dalton. “What makes you think I haven't known loss?” he asked, a flicker of pain crossing his face. “I learned the hard way that forgiveness is the only pathway to overcoming the pain.”

Dalton leaned forward, boots planted firm on the wooden floor. His jaw set, his gaze unyielding. “Forgiveness don’t fetch justice. Not out here.”

The gambler smiled thinly. He shuffled the cards absent-mindedly, each flick of the wrist a reminder of his restless mind. “Gentlemen,” he said, “revenge and redemption—they’re two sides of the same coin, and I’ve spent my life flipping it.”

He leaned back, hat tilted over his eyes, voice lowering to a confessional hush. “I once tracked a man who cheated me out of a year’s winnings. Found him in a saloon in Yuma, nursing a bottle. I could’ve shot him in the back; most wouldn’t have blamed me. But I sat down and beat him fair and square at cards instead. My revenge, he walked away a lot poorer than when he sat down.”

The preacher considered Lucky’s story. “You faced him, but what did you gain, truly?”

Lucky grinned. “A pocket full of money and a good story to tell when the whiskey runs dry.”

The stagecoach rattled on, the conversation growing deeper as the afternoon wore on. Dalton’s voice grew rough. “Preacher, don’t the Good Book say ‘an eye for an eye’? Folks out here live by simple rules. If you’re wronged, you right it.”

The preacher shook his head gently. “That was written for times when folks needed justice. But the Lord came to show us a new way—turn the other cheek. You don’t have to let evil win, but you don’t have to let it ruin you either. Forgiveness is a mighty weapon.”

Lucky tapped his cards against his knee. “Forgiveness is fine when you’re the one hurt. But what about when you’re the one who’s done wrong? Redemption’s a heavy prize. I’ve made enemies, sure as you have. Sometimes, I wonder if I’ll ever truly pay my debts.”

Dalton looked at Lucky, “You ever tried making things right?”

He shrugged. “A few times. Some folks forgive. Some don’t. Maybe it’s the trying that matters.”

The stagecoach slowed as it neared its destination, a small town on the edge of nowhere. The preacher gathered his Bible, Dalton checked the revolvers at his hip, and Lucky straightened his coat. They stepped out, each carrying unspoken burdens.

On the dusty street, the preacher turned and spoke quietly. “Remember, every man can choose. Revenge is a road without end, but redemption... It's a journey home."

After stretching his legs, Dalton climbed back into the coach and sat by the window as new passengers boarded and took their places on the narrow bench. The coach drove out towards Missouri. The preacher and his sermon long forgotten.

After weeks on the road, the stagecoach drew near to St. Louis. The church spires and the bustling riverfront signaled the end of the journey.

Dalton disembarked at the Wells Fargo office, reclaiming his saddle and walking to the outskirts of the city, where he purchased his new horse. He ran calloused hands along the animal's neck, a spirited fella, fresh from the auction yard.

With practiced ease, he slid the saddle onto the chestnut gelding's back and tightened the cinches. Bridle and bit came next, the horse tossing its head for a moment before settling. Dalton checked the stirrups, packed his bedroll, placed a battered canteen over the saddle horn, and rode out—St. Louis behind him, Springfield ahead.

Chapter 16

Piedmont, Missouri

The morning sun had scarcely lifted over the sleepy railroad boomtown of Piedmont when Dalton rode at a slow pace down Main Street. The town was already bustling with activity, and businesses on both sides were preparing for the day.

On one side, the wooden sign of the general store creaked softly in the morning breeze as customers entered. A few doors down, the postmaster sat at a window, sorting mail and arranging parcels on a worn oak counter. The last building was the sheriff's office.

Across the dusty road, the blacksmith stoked the forge, coaxing embers into a roaring fire. And further down, a man quickly swept the wooden platform as passengers gathered for the train.

The ride from St. Louis had been long and hard. Stomach growling, he hoped to find a place to get a good meal and a stiff drink before continuing to Springfield. Dalton tied his horse to the hitching post outside the one tavern in town, a two-story weather-beaten structure bordering the train station.

The air was thick with pipe smoke and the murmur of conversation punctuated by the clink of glasses. Ranch hands, drifters, and the odd well-dressed traveler sat at battered tables or stood at the bar.

Dalton chose an empty table near the door, allowing him to keep an eye on both the street and the saloon patrons at the same time. Listening and watching, he ate the bowl of warm beans and a slice of cornbread, washing it down with a few shots of whiskey. No one took notice of him. He was just one more man passing through the quiet town.

That calm was shattered when the barkeep slammed his palm on the wooden counter, demanding attention. His voice, rough as gravel, cut through the haze like a whip crack. "Fellas, listen up!

There's been a train robbery—at Gads Hill station, not more'n an hour ago. Sheriff Timberlake gathern' a posse."

In an instant, the bar erupted. Men leapt from their stools, some knocking them over with a crash, and the air thickened with the scent of spilled beer. The rattle of boots on rough floorboards drowned shouted questions, "Who did it? How many?"

A woman in a red dress paused just long enough to snatch her shawl, her glance darting between the emptied tables and the door swinging wildly on its hinges behind. She watched Dalton as he strode to his horse and swung into the saddle.

At one card table, a gambler with a voice like silk tried to lighten the mood, "Well, gentlemen, looks like the stakes just got higher. Shall we wager on how long before those bandits get caught?"

Word spread like wildfire, and a restless crowd gathered in front of the sheriff's brick-walled headquarters. Timberlake, a man with eyes as sharp as tacks, stood on the wooden stoop outside the jail, his thumbs hooked just beneath his gun belt, and said, "Reckon you've heard the news. The James Gang made off with the Gads Hill takings."

Timberlake wasted no time. The Gads Hill robbery was an insult that demanded swift justice. Timberlake's reputation as a lawman was on the line, and he was determined not to let these outlaws disappear into the Missouri wilds.

He'd already conscripted a tight-knit band of deputies, trackers, and a few local men. He turned to the crowd and pointed to several men. "You, Markham. Tully. Jones. You're deputized, too. Get your rifles and meet at the livery in ten minutes."

Eyes searching the crowd one more time, Timberlake paused as a solitary rider emerged from the dust haze at the eastern edge of Main

Street, heading out of town. The crowd parted for the tall figure astride a chestnut gelding. Two gleaming Colt revolvers hung low at his hips, the holsters slung for a quick draw.

Timberlake's gaze locked with Dalton's, and he said, "I need good men—fast men. I'm deputizing you on the spot."

Dalton's fingers twitched on the reins, restless and uneasy, and reluctantly gave a curt nod. This was not his fight; he had his own outlaws to hunt down, but he saw no way out.

Turning back to his posse, Timberlake said, "We're headed northwest; it's believed the James Gang is headed for the Meramec Caverns.

Boots thudded, and spurs rang as Timberlake issued orders with calm authority. "Saddle up. Pack light. We ride hard and fast."

Within minutes, horses stamped and snorted, deputies checked their arms. Sheriff Timberlake swung into the saddle, and the posse rode out. The chase was on, and the wild hills of Missouri echoed with the thunder of galloping hooves and the promise that Jesse James and his notorious gang would not escape justice this time.

Chapter 17

Meramec Caverns, Missouri

Dalton rode alongside the sheriff, the dust curling up around the horses' hooves. Every beat of the saddle was a reminder: this hunt was not his own.

Timberlake may have handed him the badge, temporarily turning outlaw into lawman, but Dalton's heart was far from the righteous pursuit of the James Gang. His mind drifted to his own unfinished business—the debt yet unpaid, the score unsettled. Each mile took him further from what mattered.

The terrain between Gads Hill and Meramec Caverns was no friend to the posse. The land rose and fell in a patchwork of rolling hills, tangled undergrowth, and oak forests that muffled the sound of hoofbeats. At times, the only evidence of the outlaw's passage was a freshly broken branch.

Dalton kept his eyes on the horizon, scanning for movement, listening to the wind for clues. Beneath his stoic exterior, he was planning, not for the chase, but for how he might turn it to his own advantage. If the train robbers were caught and cornered, perhaps he could slip away in the chaos.

The chase wound on for days. The outlaw gang, knowing every deer path and hidden holler, used their knowledge of the land to their benefit. At times, they doubled back on their own tracks, leading the posse in dizzying circles. Finally, the lawmen found themselves at the edge of a deep ravine, only to spot the outlaws' trail reemerging half a mile upstream.

Tension began to fray the nerves of the pursuers. Supplies dwindled. Tempers flared around the evening fires. Yet Sheriff Timberlake's determination never wavered. "They may outfox us for a night or two," he told his men, "but even the slickest varmint has to sleep sometime."

Dalton listened, resentment simmering. He thought of the badge—the symbol of a world he did not believe in. He was forced to play lawman in a game not of his making.

The men he rode with trusted him, but Dalton trusted only himself. He rode, not for justice, but for the hope that soon, very soon, he would be free to chase the ghosts that matter to him.

On the fourth day, the posse discovered a saddlebag torn and discarded at the edge of a bluff. Inside, they found a single gold pocket watch, the property of Mr. Elijah Tuttle, a passenger robbed at Gads Hill. The sight of it stoked their resolve.

Sheriff Timberlake proclaimed, “The James Gang’s close.”

As the lawmen drew nearer to Meramec Caverns, the landscape shifted. The hills grew steeper, the forests deeper. The Meramec River cut through limestone bluffs, creating gorges and shadowed hollers. It was outlaw country: wild, ungovernable, and riddled with caves.

Local legend held that Meramec Caverns, with its twisted passages and secret chambers, had served for centuries as a haven for thieves and renegades. The James Gang, clever in their choice of hideout, melted into the caverns’ darkness as the posse approached.

Sheriff Timberlake ordered his men to fan out along the riverbank, searching for signs of the fugitives’ entrance before nightfall.

Near dark, Dalton found what they needed: a scrap of red bandana snagged on a jagged rock, and boot prints leading into a narrow crack in the cliff face—the entrance.

The sheriff and his men gathered at the mouth of the cavern, lanterns raised, peering into the inky black. The outlaws, somewhere within the maze of hidden chambers, waited in silence, their revolvers cocked, their eyes accustomed to the darkness.

Quickly realizing the caverns favored the hunted over the hunters and wary of an ambush in the twisting tunnels, Timberlake hesitated to follow. “Make camp, men. We’ll wait for sunup to enter the cave.”

Horses snorted impatiently at their tethers in the growing darkness. The men built a camp near the entrance, posting sentries and keeping a watchful eye on the shadowed opening. Silence pressed in, broken only by the occasional crackle of the campfire.

Tension rose with every passing hour, and men began to talk to calm their nerves. Some wondered aloud what would happen if the gang attempted a desperate escape through one of the secret exits the cave was rumored to offer. Others questioned whether the outlaws might simply vanish without a trace.

A man Dalton came to know as Eli spoke up first. “Heard they nabbed two strongboxes, and the conductor claims Jesse himself tipped his hat before he hopped off the train.”

A man in a beaten wide-brim hat named Josiah declared, “Never seen the law make him nervous, not even with a dozen rifles aimed his way.”

Eli stirred the fire and said, “I can’t help but admire the nerve it takes to stand in the open, rob a train, and ride out under the marshal’s nose.”

Josiah asked, “You ever think about how this ends, Eli? What do we do if we catch ‘em? Jesse’s killed men before–he won’t come quietly.”

Eli paused before answering, then said, “I think about it plenty. But, I took an oath to uphold the law, no matter who stands on the other side. Besides, every time they rob a train or a bank, it makes life harder for folks like us. It's not about glory—it's about justice."

The sheriff shut down the fireside chat. "Boys, get some rest, and keep your revolvers close."

At sunrise, Sheriff Timberlake's men gathered the courage to plunge into the winding tunnels, but it was too late. The James Gang had evaded capture once more.

Under the cover of darkness, they slipped through hidden passages to the far side of the caverns. Mounting fresh horses stashed there for a quick getaway, they vanished into the wilds of the Ozark hills.

Sheriff Timberlake gathered his posse at the cave entrance. "Men, we did our best."

Eli couldn't hold back and said, "But our best wasn't good enough. Folks back home will only remember that Jessie and his men got away with the Gads Hill Train robbery."

Sheriff Timberlake replied, "You're right about that. Folks remember the outlaws, but the ones who hunt or bring 'em in rarely make the history books."

Finally free from his job as reluctant deputy, Dalton spurred his horse and galloped south to Springfield.

Chapter 18

Springfield, Missouri

In the late afternoon sun, townsfolk gathered for the annual shooting contest, which drew spectators and contestants from all around Springfield. Dust stirred by the boots of onlookers as they crowded around the makeshift shooting range on the street outside McSweeny's General Store.

Among the competitors was Dalton, who had arrived a few hours before curious onlookers began to line the street and walkways for the much-anticipated event. Pockets empty, save for a few coins and the remnants of last night's tobacco, Dalton signed his name on the contest registry. This was not just any shooting contest. The winner was promised a purse of gold coins.

His gaze wandered to the other end of the

range. There stood a slender, sharp-eyed young woman in buckskin trousers and a fringed jacket, loading cartridges into a rifle.

Some snickered at the idea—a woman in a man's contest—but others watched in silence, seeing something dangerous and wild in the way she moved, the unbending line of her jaw. She was the only woman among a sea of men, but she wore her confidence like a badge.

McSweeny, a thick-mustached man, called the competitors to line up. The contest unfolded in rounds. Cowboys, sharpshooters, and gamblers step forward. Each received a moment in the spotlight while onlookers wagered pennies and cheered for the contestants. With each round, shooters were eliminated until only two remained.

"We'll shoot three rounds. First, bottles at twenty paces. Then, coins tossed in the air. Third, the bullseye—one shot only, fifty paces. May the best marksman win!"

Dalton tipped his hat to the young woman as they took their marks. "Name's Dalton Parnell, ma'am," he said, politely with a smile.

She flashed a quick, lopsided grin. "Call me Jane," she replied, her voice husky and sure.

"Ladies first," Dalton drawled.

Jane took her position; feet planted with quiet confidence as McSweeny lined up the six glass bottles.

She drew her revolver with a speed that surprised the crowd. In the span of a heartbeat, six shots rang out, each bottle shattering in turn, glass raining to the ground with precision so perfect that the crowd stood stunned.

Dalton's grin faltered, but he stepped up, steady and practiced. Six shots later, six bottles fell, but one wobbled a moment before shattering—a fraction slower, a touch less sure.

The crowd murmured, sensing a shift in the air.

Round two arrived. McSweeny produced a handful of coins and tossed them high. Dalton fired first, three coins spinning, two falling ruined, one plinking to the sand untouched. He frowned, flicking sweat from his brow.

Jane's turn came. Her shots sang through the air; three coins, three holes, the pieces falling in perfect halves. The crowd roared, hats waved, boots stamped the earth.

Dalton squared his shoulders as the final round approached. The bullseye—a small painted circle nailed to a post, fifty paces down the street. He walked the distance, paused, aimed, and fired. The shot struck just shy of the circle's edge, a near miss that drew a gasp from the crowd.

Jane advanced, her step light, revolver spun with a flash of silver. She took aim—calm, unhurried, as if the world had slowed—and squeezed the trigger. The bullet struck dead center, splitting the bullseye with a crack so sharp it echoed down the silent street.

The contest was decided. The crowd surged forward, eager to know the identity of this mysterious woman with the quick draw.

The contest promoter handed the bag of coins over to Jane. "Ma'am, you shoot like you've spent your life in the saddle. What's your name?"

The winner tipped her hat back, revealing a mane of sandy hair. She smiled, the hint of wildness in her manner now fully unfurled. "They call me Calamity Jane," she said, her voice ringing with pride and a touch of mischief.

Recognition swept the crowd in a wave. Stories of Calamity Jane had long traveled the Missouri trails—her exploits with Wild Bill Hickok, her daring rides, her quick temper, and quicker draw.

Dalton, chastened but not bitter, stepped forward and tipped his hat in genuine respect. "Well, Miss Jane, I reckon I just got schooled proper. Ain't every day you lose to a legend."

Calamity Jane grinned, her laughter bubbling up like spring water. "It's all in the wrist, Dalton, plus a little luck."

Dalton tipped his hat and pushed his way through the crowd gathering around Jane. He needed a room for the night and a seat at a poker table, where he hoped "Lady Luck" might look kindly on a cowboy down on his luck.

Chapter 19

Springfield, Missouri

Around noon, Dalton appeared on the southeast corner of Springfield's public square. He spied Rusty on the opposite corner, strutting around, showing off his late-night poker winnings, Dalton's prized pocket watch.

"I warned you!" Dalton's voice carried across the distance to the man.

Spotting Dalton, Rusty laughed, revealing uneven, yellow teeth. With a taunting sneer, he flipped the silver lid on the timepiece, making a big show of checking the hour. The gesture enraged Dalton.

The night before, Dalton, several tinhorns, and a cowboy they called Rusty sat gambling in the Lyon Hotel, which was located one block north of the square on South Street. Dalton had not forgotten the man or his ruthless deeds. He had pursued the outlaw and the other Kansas raiders through stretches of prairies and narrow valleys nestled between hills or ridges. Still, his resolve never waned. The taste of justice drove him onward, each mile bringing him closer to this moment of reckoning.

It was his good fortune that the outlaw hadn't recognized him as the gunman who killed three of his partners that night at the Bull Head Saloon in Abilene, Kansas. He had no idea that the man who had chased him across the West now sat at the green felt table, planning how to kill him.

Dalton was a good poker player. He prided himself on being able to outsmart the other gamblers, but not on this night. Lady Luck was not on his side. Rusty had cleaned him out. By the end of the game, Dalton owed the man $25.

Foolishly, he'd put his father's watch up as collateral until he could pay off the debt. However, he issued a warning before leaving the table, "Don't be flashing that watch and bragging 'bout taking it from me."

Of course, Rusty, being a natural braggart, couldn't resist the temptation of boasting about the card game and his winnings. Drawing a sizable crowd to hear the story, hoping to humiliate Dalton further, he detailed the play-by-play action of the night before.

Alerted to trouble by an elbow in the ribs, Rusty paused and scoured the area as the crowd headed for cover. It didn't take long to identify the cause. Recognizing the white canvas duster and black Stetson, he sneered and headed for the man.

"Don't cross over," Dalton warned.

Instead of heeding the warning, Rusty continued, drawing his revolver and firing.

It was then that Dalton drew the Colt and fired from a distance of seventy-five yards, shooting his opponent.

As Dalton bent to scoop the silver watch from the dead man's hand, he heard an eyewitness to the gunfight exclaim, "That was one hell of a shot, mister!"

Later, the coroner would report. "Straight through the heart."

Chapter 20

Southwest Missouri

The morning sun painted the rolling hills south of Springfield in shades of gold and copper. The chatter of katydids hung low over the green valley as a hawk circled in the gentle fall breeze.

Dalton sat astride the gelding atop one of these hills. His hat, battered by wind and rain, pulled low, cast a shadow over his steel-gray eyes, which had hardened from long miles and a thirst for revenge.

In his hand, he toyed with the reins, feeling the horse's quiet patience. Out of money, he needed a place to lie low for a while after the shootout on the square in Springfield put him in the crosshairs of the law.

Below him sprawled the Bar Z cattle ranch. A herd of beefy, dark-coated cattle wandered through short pine and oak near a creek bed, flicking flies from their backs with lazy tails. Smoke curled from the chimney of the ranch house, ringed by a wooden fence that created a barrier between the barn, sheds, and bunkhouse nearby. In the distance, a pair of cowhands moved with practiced ease, mending a section of board fencing.

Roy Conrad's words echoed in his mind, from months ago when wagon wheels rattled across the vast Texas prairie. "If you ever make it back East, son, look up my brother-in-law, Simon Woodlee, at the Bar Z. Tell him Roy sent you. It's good land, good people. They'll need another hand come spring."

At the memory, a faint smile tugged at the corners of the cowboy's mouth. He patted the horse's neck. "Let's see if Roy's word still carries weight, old boy," he murmured.

Dalton urged the gelding forward with a gentle nudge of his heels. The descent was easy, the grass parting beneath iron-shod hooves. By the time he reached the ranch gate, a tall man, hair streaked with silver, was already striding out from the porch. His eyes, shrewd and steady, met the cowboy's with a mixture of curiosity and calculation.

Dalton dismounted, dusted off his pants, and led the horse forward. He didn't bother rehearsing his words—out here, a man's story was measured more by his handshake than his speech.

"Afternoon. Name's Dalton Parnell. I rode west with Roy Conrad on the wagon train headed to Santa Fe. He said if I ever came this way, I might find work at the Bar Z."

Simon's face softened a fraction at the mention of Roy's name. He took in the lean build, the sure hands, the sun-browned face, and the two pearl-handled Colts strapped to his waist—a man who'd seen his share of hard work and danger. One that could be counted on when a herd stampeded and when trouble rode in.

"Roy Conrad, you say?" Simon asked, voice gravelly with years. "Haven't seen Roy in near two springs, but his word still counts for something around here. What brings you out this way?"

Dalton looked past the rancher, letting his eyes sweep the expanse of land—the cattle, the house, the hope of finding Morgan. "I've driven cattle along the Chisholm. Learned my way around a branding fire and a round-up, but I'm looking to settle, maybe put down roots. Roy said you might need another pair of hands."

Simon nodded, rubbing his chin. "Always need good men, though the work is rough and the pay's honest, but not much more."

Dalton grinned, the first real warmth since crossing the border into Missouri. "Better than my seat at a poker table, and I've kept more than one greenhorn from getting run over at a stampede."

A laugh escaped Simon. "That'll do. We've got a stubborn herd and a fence line that never seems to hold. You'll find the bunkhouse behind the main barn. Suppers at sundown."

Dalton nodded, gratitude flickering behind his steady gaze. “Thank you, Mr. Woodlee. I won’t let you down.”

Simon offered a hand. Dalton took it. “Welcome to the Bar Z, Parnell.”

Pulling at the reins, Dalton guided the gelding toward the corral. He exchanged nods with the other ranch hands, their eyes sizing up the newcomer, their greetings reserved but not unfriendly. He stabled his horse, rubbing its nose and promising oats later.

Dalton was met by a stable hand. The old man thumbed his belt while staring at Dalton’s holsters. “Don’t see many folks wearing irons like that unless they aim to use ‘em,” he muttered.

Several ranch hands watched from under the brims of their hats, their chatter dying to a hush as Dalton passed on his way to the bunkhouse. There was an unspoken rule out on the open range. Folks carried rifles slung over their shoulders for coyotes and the occasional copperhead, but pistols—let alone two—meant the bearer kept company with trouble, or trouble kept company with them.

Inside the bunkhouse, the air was filled with the scent of leather, tobacco smoke, and the lingering musk of sweat and wool. Dalton tossed the saddlebags on one of the empty bunks lining the walls. He lay back on the straw mattresses, covered with a heavy wool blanket, and rested his head on the horsehair pillow and waited. It wasn’t long before the bunkhouse was filled with men, dusty and tired.

Chapter 21

Southwest Missouri

Before sunset, Dalton and the other cowhands began their slow migration back toward the bunkhouse. Each man moved at their own pace, some walking together in pairs, others like Dalton trailing silently behind.

The hard day on the range, wrangling cattle and mending fences, had finally come to an end. Dust clung to their jeans and boots; the creases of their sunburned faces marked by sweat and grit.

The men enter the bunkhouse. The sounds of heavy boots on worn boards announce that their day's work was done. Hats removed, dust shaken free, they were met with the cook stirring a pot of brown beans on the stove. The aroma mingled with the strong, black coffee that had brewed all day.

Some left briefly to tend to the final chores—filling the water troughs and making sure the gates were secure. Others lingered in the kitchen, drawn by the warmth of food and the promise of a well-earned meal.

When the meal was finally served, everyone gathered around the table. Plates were passed, hands reached across the table for slices of cornbread, and the conversation turned from work to the world beyond the ranch.

After supper, the men stretched out on their bunks, boots off, eyes heavy. The hum of conversation faded, replaced by the rustle of blankets and the steady breathing of those who slept.

The quiet was broken when Simon Woodlee strode through the door, boots ringing out against the worn floorboards, hat in hand, a glint in his eyes. The men looked up in surprise. The boss rarely ventured into the bunkhouse at the day's end unless there was something important to say.

"Listen up, boys," the boss called, his voice carrying a hint of mischief. "Towns got itself a carnival tonight—lights, tents, the whole shebang. Figured y'all earned a good night out. Ranch work's done, and I won't hear of any of you stickin' round here. You've got the night off."

For a heartbeat, the words hovered in the air, then the room erupted. Boots thumped against floorboards, bunks rattled as men leapt to their feet, and whoops rang out.

"Hot damn!" hollered Clay, the youngest

hand, his grin as wide as an open prairie. He wrenched his hat off the nail and spun it in the air, nearly colliding with Old Jeb, who chuckled and clapped him on the back.

"Imagine that. Carnival night in town!" Old Jeb chuckled. "Haven't been to a real carnival since I was knee-high to a grasshopper."

Dalton lay on his bed, head propped up on the pillow as men dashed to their bunks to dig out clean shirts and their Sunday boots, hidden away for just such special occasions. Laughter and teasing filled the air. A good-natured ribbing broke out among the men about who would win the biggest stuffed bear for a sweetheart and who'd spend all their wages on games and come home empty-handed.

At the washstand, men took turns scrubbing their faces in cold water, washing away the day's grime and fatigue. Mirrors were propped up on windowsills, and the business of getting presentable took a serious turn.

The bunkhouse, usually echoing with snores at this time of day, was alive with a rare energy. A carnival night was enough to erase the ache of tired muscles and the dust of a week's hard work.

Some shouted out plans, "First round of lemonade's on me!" Others threatened friendly revenge at the dunk tank. Even Dalton found himself swept up in the carnival excitement, and a broad smile broke through his usual indifference.

The men spilled out into the twilight, the Bar Z behind them. Dalton joined the group as they mounted up and rode out. The heat and dust of the day, forgotten. Tonight, work, worry, and revenge were swapped for laughter, bright lights, and the magic of a carnival.

CHAPTER 22

Springfield, Missouri

Dalton and the ranch hands were greeted with the aroma of roasting corn and sweet molasses as they entered Springfield. The main square bustled with townsfolk, farmers, and cowboys. Stepping away from their horses, dusting off their hats, the Bar Z men grinned at the lively scene.

Old Jeb said, "Well, boys, wouldn't you look at that. Folks from all over the county must've come out this year."

Taking the lead, he wove a trail through a throng of townsfolk. Children darted between carnival goers' legs. Women in calico dresses fanned themselves on the boardwalk while old-timers with pipes swapped stories on hay bales lining the street.

Old Jeb briefly stopped in front of a line of

tents housing traveling performers. At one, a bearded lady astonished crowds with feats of strength. At another, a magician, in a faded velvet coat, conjured coins from behind children's ears. Hearing carnival barkers call out invitations to test one's strength and skills or try luck at games of chance, he quickly moved on.

Dalton smiled. Here's what the ranch hands had come for: a chance to show off, win money, and earn bragging rights until the next carnival. Nothing to prove, he stood back and watched.

Clay let it be known, "I'm here for the shooting gallery. Want to see if I can beat Boston's record this year. He got lucky last time—wind was at his back."

The ranch hands chuckled when Old Jeb said, "Or maybe you just can't shoot straight after dark, Kid."

Taking no offense at the good-hearted ribbing, Clay stepped up, took aim at spinning tin targets, six-shooters flashing in the dark. Cheers erupted each time a mark was shattered.

His old friend and the other Bar Z men goaded each other into taking a chance. A few finally took the bait and lined up, hoping to beat Clay's record and win the silver belt buckle.

Others went on to the roping booth. The onlookers gasped as the loops sailed through the air with practiced grace, the best snaring the horns of wooden steers. A few moved on to the axe-throwing booth and hurled blades at painted bullseyes, earning the admiration of the gathering crowd.

Dalton leaned against the painted boards of the shooting gallery. Boots planted firmly in the churned earth, spurs motionless, his eyes never settling in one place for long.

He watched the crowd with the practiced patience of a hunter—tracking not deer nor coyote, but for men. If any member of Morgan's gang of outlaws were foolish enough to attend the carnival, they would regret it.

Curiosity drew Dalton's eyes to the edge of the bustling carnival. There stood a tent unlike any other, wrapped in deep purple velvet that shimmered like starlight. Gold embroidery traced constellations across the canvas, their patterns catching the flickering lantern-light. Across the tent's entrance, a sign hung—"Madame Zahara: Seer of Truths, Whisperer of Fates."

Some carnival-goers paused at the tent, attracted to the candles flickering in glass jars, while others, making the sign of the cross, passed by quickly. Dalton showed no hesitation. Drawn by the strange magnetism of the unknown. The fortune teller's tent, with its promise of answers, beckoned like a dare.

He pushed aside the beaded curtain, and the noise outside faded to a muffled hum. The jingle announced his arrival as he stepped into the candlelit tent. Burning incense floated gently in the air as if trying to calm an unseen world of restless spirits.

In the very center sat a low, round table draped in red silk; upon its surface rested a crystal ball. Beside the ball, a deck of cards lay spread in a fan, each worn at the edges, its colors faded, but its images, vivid. A single lamp, shaped like a crescent moon, glowed softly.

The gypsy, Madame Zahara, sat poised behind the table, half-shrouded in shadows, dark eyes gleaming with the reflection of candlelight. Dressed in layers of flowing silks and scarves, adorned with a cascade of beads and bangles, she waited.

With one single wave of a hand, she invited her guest to sit. She studied the cowboy, hat tipped low to shield his eyes from the lamplight, as he sat, resting his elbows on the weathered table between them.

Smoothing silky waves of dark hair from her face, the fortune teller gracefully shuffled the worn cards. Her eyes never left the rough-edged cowboy, guns strapped to his side, seated before her. She offered him the deck with a knowing smile.

Though he tried to disguise his purpose beneath a mask of indifference, she understood the weight that drew him here. The silent questions about choices and fate that no gunfight could resolve.

As the cards changed hands, she already knew the answers he sought. It lay not in the cards but in the depths of his own heart.

Dalton's hands hovered uncertainly, then he wrapped his fingers around the cards. Tapping them against the heel of his palm, he squared the deck, then split it into two halves. With a practiced motion, he brought the halves together, letting the cards cascade and interlace in a smooth, flowing shuffle. Satisfied, he paused, then handed the deck across the table to the gypsy.

Their hands touched; their eyes met for a few brief seconds. Madam Zahara, showing no emotion, placed the deck face down on the table and cautioned, "The future is not fixed. You can change things before they happen by heeding the message in the cards."

With one dramatic sweep, she spread the deck in a semicircle around the edge of the tabletop.

"Draw three cards and lay them face down in a row. These will answer questions about your past, present, and future." She patiently waited until the last card was in place and then said, "Let's see what wisdom the cards want to share with you today."

Her hands hovered above the three, and then turned the first, revealing a skeletal rider crossing a river beneath a blood-red sky. Zahara whispered, "Death."

Dalton's jaw clenched, but the fortune teller shook her head gently.

"Death is not only an ending," she revealed, "but a beginning. You rode a trail that was marked with endings before you ever saddled your horse."

Flipping the second card, a tower, struck by lightning, its stone walls crumbling, she lay beside Death. "You seek to destroy what destroyed you. Justice and vengeance ride side by side, but their trails separate at the fork in the road."

The third card showed a man suspended upside down. The dark-eyed gypsy softly named it, "The Hanged Man." She paused for a moment, then advised, "You will be forced to see the world through different eyes. Patience and sacrifice will be demanded, but if you hold fast only to anger, your journey will end in sorrow."

The reading ended, and Madame Zahara smiled, sitting back.

When the cowboy went to place a few coins on the table, she grabbed his hand and cautioned, "Remember, the West is wide, but a man's heart is wider still. What you choose to carry will follow you, long after your enemies are dust."

As Dalton pulled aside the velvet curtain, the fortune teller's voice followed him out into the night. "You will walk the knife's edge between justice and vengeance, and the sharpest wound may be to your own soul."

Chapter 23

Southwest Missouri

As the sun peeked over the hillside, the Bar Z Ranch stood poised for the barn raising. Word of the event had traveled swiftly, reaching every homestead within a day's horseback ride. Soon, neighbors, their families, and any able-bodied men in the county would arrive willing to lend a hand.

The men of the Bar Z had risen early after the night of fun at the carnival. Gathering in front of the corral, the foreman organized the men. The most experienced were tasked with guiding the placement of joists; others hefted lumber, hammered nails, or braced ladders.

Throughout the morning hours, men and women arrived in steady streams, their wagons creaking under the weight of timber. Women carried baskets brimming with flaky pies, tins of roasted meats, beans stewed overnight, and fresh-baked bread. Men on horseback arrived with tools slung over their shoulders, battered hammers and saws shoved into saddle bags.

Dalton was unloading a stack of beams with a few other ranch hands when the soft clatter of a wagon drew his gaze. He paused and watched as a weathered but sturdy wagon rolled up the path, its wheels trailing curls of dust.

Atop the wagon sat a family, a man in a faded hat, his wife beside him, and between them, a young woman. As the wagon drew nearer, the sunlight caught on the crisp white of her cotton bonnet and the stray wisps of honey-blonde hair curling her cheeks.

Her father guided the horses to a halt near the workers. The wagon bed was stacked with rough-cut planks, lengths of fresh oak. Dalton's gaze lingered on the girl as she reached first for her father's steady arm, then for the bundles they had brought.

For a moment, time seemed to slow: the calls of the men, the laughter of the women, the whinny of horses—all faded to a gentle murmur. Her bonnet's ribbons fluttered in the breeze as bright blue eyes glanced his way.

Dalton managed a slight nod. And returned to his work.

As the morning wore on, he worked alongside neighbors and ranch hands as the barn beams rose on all sides. Yet, every so often, he found his thoughts drifting to the blue-eyed girl in the bonnet.

Dalton was working on bracing the western

wall when he noticed her approach. A strand of hair had slipped free of the bonnet, and she tucked it behind her ear. In her arms, she carried a small bucket of nails. As she drew near, Dalton straightened from his crouch, wiping his brow with the back of his hand.

"Could you use some of these?" she asked, voice gentle but clear.

He nodded, momentarily tongue-tied. Her eyes—now revealed to be flecked with green—regarded him with quiet amusement.

"Thank you," he said, grabbing a handful from the bucket.

"My name's Clara," she offered, setting the pail down. "My folks are the Whitmans, from up near Flat Creek."

"Dalton," he replied, almost tripping over his own name. "Glad to meet you, Miss Clara."

She smiled, grabbed the bucket handle, and walked on, asking each man with a hammer the same question.

Throughout the day, Dalton and Clara crossed paths again and again—sometimes by chance, and sometimes Dalton suspected, by quiet design. Her bonnet askew and cheeks flushed, she would wink and give him a flirty smile. As the day heated up, she helped the other young women fetch water for the thirsty builders. She was always the first to offer Dalton a drink.

At day's end, the frame of the barn stood tall against the evening sky. The air, thick with the scent of fresh bread and roasting meat, signaled everyone to gather for supper.

Dalton found himself seated near Clara and her parents. Stories were exchanged, plans for next year's harvest discussed, and Dalton felt warmth in his chest that had little to do with the hearty stew in his bowl.

At dusk, the neighbors began to drift homeward. The Whitmans loaded the last of their tools, preparing for the journey back along the rutted country road. Dalton helped Clara's father secure a loose board atop the wagon, earning a grateful nod and a firm handshake.

Clara, already seated beside her mother, offered Dalton one last smile—a promise, perhaps, of conversations yet to come. A strand of blonde hair fluttered in the soft evening breeze as the wagon rolled away, fading from sight.

Dalton lingered by the new barn, the scent and memory of Clara's laughter lingering in the air. He knew he would not forget the girl in the bonnet, nor the day when the world seemed, for a moment, to offer a new beginning.

He leaned against a splintered fence rail, his hat tilted low, as he appeared to watch the wagon roll down the trail home. In truth, his ears strained to catch the voices from behind the tool shed, where two weather-beaten ranchers stood loading their wagons to head home.

All thoughts of the young woman vanished as their voices, rough and deep, carried on the wind—just enough for Dalton to catch what was being said. "Never seen nothin' like it," drawled the taller man. "Whole herd gone before sunrise. And Sam's boy, shot clean through the shoulder. Ain't right."

His companion spat into the dust, eyes scanning the endless Missouri valley. "That band of rustlers ain't satisfied with cattle. They ran off with six head from the Miller place, and poor Hank's still laid up in bed. Sheriff's got no lead, and folks are scared."

"Heard the rustlers are from Kansas, led by a ruthless outlaw named John Morgan. Word is, they're held up just south of here in Stone County."

Dalton's chest tightened. The names and stories matched the rumors drifting through grimy saloons in Springfield. Ranch hands gunned down in the dark, cattle vanishing as if the earth had swallowed them whole.

He pressed his palm against the cool, sun-bleached wood, piecing together what the ranchers revealed. The very information Dalton had hoped to find when he'd strolled up to Simon Woodlee, offering his hand and his horse in return for a job.

Dalton's jaw set. He tipped his hat lower and slipped away before the ranchers could spot him. For Dalton, the time for listening was over. The time for action would soon be at hand.

Chapter 24

Southwest Missouri

Barn built, Simon Woodlee declared a "barn warming"—a tradition as old as the West itself. The day had been spent in preparation. By sundown, wagons rattled down the dirt lane, families perched atop hay bales, arms laden with baskets of fried chicken, pies, and jugs of cider and whiskey.

Inside the newly raised barn, guests were greeted by the sounds of laughter, fiddles, and boots stomping. Lanterns hung from the rafters cast golden pools of light over the crowd, and the scent of roasting beef mingled with the sweet tang of apple cider.

Yet, in the shadows near the open doorway, Dalton lingered, a careful observer amid the merriment. He hadn't come solely for the dance or the spread—though both were fine as any he'd seen—but for whispers. Information had a way of slipping out when men's tongues were loosened by warmth and whiskey, and Dalton, new to the Bar Z outfit, had a knack for listening.

He stood back in the shadows near the open barn door, leaning against a post. His hat pulled low, casting his eyes in shadow, but he missed nothing. He watched as neighbors greeted neighbors, old rivalries set aside for a night of fellowship. Plates piled high with food passed from hand to hand, laughter spilling like water over the dance floor.

In one corner, atop a makeshift platform of crates, the band struck up a merry tune. The fiddler's bow flashed in the lamplight. Beside him, a banjo player plucked at silver strings, his fingers nimble and sure. A sturdy man with a jaw harp joined in while the beat of the tune was kept steady by the stomp of boots, the thud of wooden spoons, and the strumming of the washboard player.

They entertained with jigs and ballads passed down through generations. Tunes like "Soldier's Joy" and "Turkey in the Straw" ripple through the barn, each piece played with infectious energy and the occasional offbeat holler from the fiddler. The music flowed easily from one tune to the next, never ceasing for long, for the aim was to keep feet moving and spirits high.

The barn floor, swept clean and lit by flickering oil lamps, became a stage for lively dance. Young and old, men and women, partners and friends, all took to the floor guided by the caller shouting above the music: "Swing your partner!"

There was laughter and the shuffle of boots as dancers whirled. Arms interlocked, skirts and petticoats flew, and suspenders snapped. Children darted between the dancers, mimicking their steps, while old folks clapped from the sidelines.

Between sets, the dancers paused to catch their breath, wiping brows with handkerchiefs, fanning faces, or sipping cider from tin cups. But as soon as the fiddler struck up a new tune, they returned, feet tapping, eager for another round.

Dalton's gaze swept the crowd. Tonight, he hoped to catch a rumor, a nervous glance, perhaps even one of the men involved in the rustling slipping among the shadows.

But as he watched, the door swung wide, and there stood Clara and her parents. He watched as she greeted friends with easy laughter, her blue eyes lit with excitement.

Dalton felt a jolt, unexpected and unwelcome. He had not thought of her since the barn raising. His days were filled with ranch work, and his nights were spent in the single-minded pursuit of justice. From dusk to daylight, he rode the hills and hollers of Stone County searching for the outlaws' hideout.

The band changed tunes, and the dancers parted. Dalton found himself moving forward, hat in hand, boots echoing across the floor. He offered a gentle invitation, just a dance, nothing more. She accepted with a shy smile, and together they spun into the lively circle. For a fleeting moment, Dalton let the music carry him, forgetting the weight he bore.

But the barn was alive with young men, and it wasn't long before other ranch hands—eager, grinning—cut in, taking the young woman's hand and sweeping her away into the next round. Dalton stood back, heart pounding not from the dance but from the sudden reminder of why he was here.

He retreated again to the shadows, jaw set. This was neither the time nor the place for distractions, especially those with eyes as bright as prairie sky and laughter that did strange things to a man's resolve. Dalton tipped his hat low once more, scanning the crowd.

As the barn warming celebration swelled, two ranchers, faces weathered by sun and suspicion, eased away from the crowd. They spoke in low tones, but their words carried to Dalton, who leaned on a wall just beyond a stack of hay bales.

"I heard the rustlers were spotted again, over by Flat Creek that cuts through old McAllister's land," one said, his voice fraught with a tension that contradicted the revelry inside. "Bold as brass, driving off twelve head in broad daylight."

The other spat, "Lucky that's all they got. Folks say those thieves don't just steal; they'll shoot a ranch hand without warning. Danny O'Reilly's boy got a slug in the leg last week. And two more hands are still laid up from an ambush near the south range.

One of the rustlers, wounded and desperate, had been cornered in the most unlikely of places: the chicken house. O'Reilly, flanked by his ranch hands, yanked the outlaw from his makeshift hiding spot."

"What happened to the rustler?" the first rancher asked.

"He is still swinging from that oak tree near O'Reilly's chicken house. But before the wooden bucket was kicked out from under him, he spilled his guts, thinking it would save him from the noose. Seems the leader of the rustlers has a homestead hidden in the woods not more than twenty miles from here."

The first rancher's voice dropped lower. "We're all targets, if you ask me. Sheriffs got nothing but empty words, and the Bar Z is sitting right in their path. If we don't do something..."

A burst of laughter from inside the barn put an end to the story. The two men drifted toward the light; their faces quickly masked with smiles.

Dalton didn't move, heart pounding in the dark, the weight of their words settling over him like dust after a stampede. His purpose sharpened: see justice done for the family he'd lost. For Dalton, duty called louder than even the sweetest music or the smile of the blue-eyed girl in the white bonnet.

Chapter 25

Southwest Missouri

Simon Woodlee cinched the saddle on his chestnut gelding with gloved hands, impatient to get started. This morning, however, his mind was not on cattle but on the matter of payroll. The ranch hands expected their wages on time, and Simon, a man of his word, was determined not to let his men down.

The banking business in Springfield was unreliable. The war had scattered capital, and trust in government and local institutions was fragile at best. His banker was in Liberty, nearly two hundred miles north. Making the journey to withdraw the funds he needed from his account was a simple act, fraught with the dangers of the road.

He was not a man easily given to fear, but

the postwar years had made caution a virtue. Outlaws roamed freely, and a band of rustlers was killing and stealing herds near the Bar Z. The value of a payroll was enough to tempt these desperate souls.

Desperate, Simon turned to Dalton—a man who carried his Colt revolvers with a familiarity that hinted at long nights and fast decisions. Simon trusted the new ranch hand. He knew that with Dalton at his side, the journey would be a little less uncertain.

As dawn broke, Dalton left the bunkhouse and headed to the corral where Simond waited. The two men rode. Their horses cut a brisk pace north, hooves thumping a steady rhythm on the packed earth of the trail. Dalton rode slightly behind, his gaze flicking from the tree line to the crossroads, ever watchful.

The countryside between Springfield and Liberty was a vast land of green valleys, rolling hills, and patches of oak and pine trees. Occasionally, they would meet other travelers—farmers moving supplies, women in covered wagons, the occasional drifter. Dalton nodded at these folks, but his hands never strayed far from the butt of his Colts.

At midday, the riders stopped near a creek. Simon unpacked a satchel containing cold bacon, biscuits, and a flask of strong coffee. The two men ate in silence, listening to the water and the distant call of a hawk. Dalton watched the horizon, then spoke in a voice low and even.

"Boss, you reckon words got out about your

withdrawal?" he asked, eyes scanning the brush.

Simon shrugged. "Could be. Secrets don't stay buried long in these here parts."

Dalton chewed his slice of bacon slowly. "Just as well you brought me."

After watering the horses, the two climbed into their saddles and continued the ride under a sky that threatened rain. The well-traveled trail wound northward, at times hugging riverbanks and at other times climbing steep ridges.

Dalton felt the tension mounting. Not from any specific danger, but from the realization that each mile brought its own risks.

As they neared Bolivar, a small town with a reputation for rowdy saloons, Dalton suggested they avoid the main street. Instead, they skirted the town and pressed on toward Osceola, where they lodged for the night in a ramshackle inn.

The room was cramped; the beds were hard. Dalton insisted on keeping watch while Simon slept. The next morning, they rose before the town did, slipping out quietly and resuming their ride.

North of Osceola, the land grew rougher. The innkeeper had warned that bands of former bushwhackers, their allegiance to law questionable, roamed the woods. Dalton's vigilance intensified. Once, as they passed beneath the shade of a cluster of elms, Dalton stopped abruptly.

"Rider up ahead," he murmured, signaling

for quiet.

They watched as a solitary figure approached—a farmer, it turned out, and a mule loaded with seed. The tension eased, but Dalton's sharpness never wavered.

Simon respected that. He thought about why he'd chosen the young ranch hand for this journey. It wasn't just the guns; it was the certainty—the confidence that when trouble came, Dalton wouldn't hesitate.

As the days passed, the bond between the two men deepened. Simon shared stories of his ranch, of the lost cattle during the winter storms, and of the men who'd helped rebuild after the war.

Dalton spoke little of his past. Sharing only how he came to join the wagon train traveling West and the kindness shown to him by Simon's brother-in-law.

Approaching Liberty at last, the landscape grew gentler. The Missouri River shimmered in the distance. Fields of wheat swayed in the breeze.

Dalton scanned the townsfolk who went about their errands, and the square hummed with the rhythm of everyday life. Liberty, a quiet county seat with little more than a courthouse square and brick storefronts, seemed an unlikely stage for trouble. The County Savings Association was a small but reputable institution, its modest vault holding the fortunes and savings of local merchants, farmers, and the county government.

Simon dismounted and tied his horse to the

hitching post. Dalton did the same, standing beside him, eyes alert for trouble. Inside the bank, the air was cool and still. The two approached the teller. Simon gave his name and requested the withdrawal. The process was slow—papers to sign, signatures to verify—but at last, the cashier counted out the bills and placed them in Simon's lockbox.

Chapter 26

Liberty, Missouri

Eight riders, their faces partially obscured by hats and bandanas, approached Liberty with quiet purpose. Two riders pulled the silk scarves from their faces and tethered their horses in front of the bank while the others took up positions along the street.

Giving little outward signs of their true intentions, the two entered the bank. The first man, dark-haired with a mustache and beard, approached the counter and handed the cashier a large bill, asking it to be changed.

The cashier looked at the bill and then back at the customer. Without warning, the man yanked out his pistol and shoved it into the cashier's face. The clerk, taken by surprise, raised his hands.

The gunman's partner, a thin-haired, burly

cowboy, waved his gun at Simon, Dalton, and the other customers and demanded, "Hands in the air." Seeing the lockbox Simon was holding close to his chest, the robber ordered, "Hand it over."

Dalton reached for his Colts, but Simon placed his hand on his arm and shook his head as a warning. Grudgingly, he turned the box over.

With a combination of threats and brandished revolvers, the dark-haired man demanded the contents of the safe. He handed the bank manager a large grain sack and ordered, "Put it all in the bag."

The cashier complied swiftly, stuffing $60,000 in cash, bonds, and gold coins into the sack.

Taking the sack, the robbers ordered the bank employees and customers inside the vault. Slamming the heavy steel door, the two quickly ran outside and mounted their horses.

What they didn't know was that the vault wasn't locked. The bank manager pushed it open and ran to the window. "Robbery," he yelled over and over.

As the robbers exited the bank, the alarm spread through Liberty. Local citizens, unarmed and bewildered, soon realized the magnitude of what had occurred.

The outlaws mounted their horses and prepared to make their escape, but chaos erupted in the wake of their flight.

As the bank robbers rode out of town, Dalton, Colts drawn, ran from the bank and started firing. One robber slumped in his saddle, dropping Simon's lockbox.

Dalton ran to the box and grabbed it from the ground. Handing it to Simon, he pushed his boss towards their horses as a crowd gathered outside the bank, joined by the sheriff.

"Who saw which way they went?" the sheriff barked, his voice cutting through the confusion like a whip.

"It was the James Gang. I recognized Frank James and Cole Younger from their wanted posters," a man yelled out from the back of the crowd.

A young stable boy, eyes widened, pointed northward, where the trail dipped into a shadowy stand of cottonwoods. "Out past the old mill," he stammered.

The sheriff marched to the center of town, raising his voice above the din. "We can't let those outlaws get away. Who's with me?"

Within minutes, the group swelled to a dozen. Each man brought what they could—rifles, pistols, lanterns, canteens, and horses hastily saddled.

When the posse rode out, Dalton and Simon mounted up and headed south. Dalton had no beef with the outlaws and didn't want to get in their crosshairs. He was just doing his job, protecting his boss and ensuring he returned to the ranch with payroll in hand.

Days later, Simon and Dalton arrived back at the Bar Z. Simon recounted every detail of the Liberty bank robbery to the ranch hands that met him at the corral while Dalton unsaddled his horse and headed to the bunkhouse. The story of Simon's escape with the payroll safe at his side became one told and retold around campfires for many days.

Chapter 27

Southwest Missouri

Weary from another long day on the trail, Dalton stretched out on his bedroll near one of the oak trees away from the other ranch hands. The flickering and dancing flames of the fire cast a warm, orange glow over the campsite. The smell of men, animals, and cooking hung in the air.

Dalton closed his eyes, relaxing in the smoky warmth of a crackling fire. For a week, he and the other ranch hands lived and worked outdoors, sleeping and eating under the open sky. Their days were filled with rounding up, branding, and separating the steers, getting them ready for the cattle drive to the Springfield stockyards.

The first gunshot roused Dalton as he was drifting off to sleep. He reached for his

Winchester and peered into the darkness for some sign of where the shot had come from. “Get down!” he shouted to the others in the camp, struggling with boots and gun belts.

Everyone took cover as several of the ranch hands returned fire. Dalton dropped low and took a quick look around. He had little faith that the hired hands were hitting anything so far, but at least it would keep the rustlers at bay for a little while longer.

“Put out the fire,” someone hollered at the camp cook as reports from rifles and revolvers crackled overhead.

More shots rang out, and the herd of longhorns shifted uneasily, bellowing and snorting, voicing their nervousness. Simon Woodlee called out, “Listen up, boys. I don’t know who’s shooting at us, but we need to stop it... and fast. If the herd starts running, we could lose a week trying to get ‘em back.”

“How ‘n the hell are we gonna do that while we're taking fire, Boss?” one drover demanded.

“Take care of that the best you can but keep a sharp eye on the stock while you’re about it,” the boss replied.

One ranch hand yelled, “Judging from the sounds and muzzle flashes of their firearms, there might be dozens of them.”

Witnessing the panic and confusion, of one thing Dalton was sure, the Bar Z cowhands were not gunmen; they were ranch hands. They had no experience with cattle rustlers and didn’t know how to protect the herd while fighting for their lives.

Dalton dropped to the ground and bellied his way to Simon, hunkered down behind a tree. “Boss, it only stands to reason that whoever mounted the attack has plans for the herd, and they don’t intend to stop until they get what they came for.”

Simon nodded and waited for Dalton to continue. “The Bar Z ranch hands are an obstacle. Killing us would make it easier for the rustlers to carry out their plan. One thing I learned as a drover for the JA Cattle Ranch in Texas was how to stop rustlers in their tracks. The trick is to focus on one man at a time. Once they’re dead, swiftly move on to the next target.”

Simon considered what had been said. Dalton had proven to be a hard worker who knew a great deal about ranching. Convinced the cowhand knew what he was talking about, he shook his head in agreement and yelled, “Okay, boys, shoot to kill. We’re not lawmen, so don’t bother trying to take any prisoners.”

A scream from nearby put an end to talking, and both men turned toward the sound. One of the Bar Z men had fallen near the chuck wagon. Dalton ran to the wagon and nudged the limp man with his foot.

Getting no response, he knelt and rolled over the dead body. It was the camp cook. A bullet had pierced his lungs. Dalton reckoned the Bar Z would be lucky if the cook proved to be the only man lost to the rustlers.

He had learned a thing or two driving cattle across Texas to Abilene, Kansas. First and foremost, when dealing with rustlers or Indians, it was kill or be killed. And one thing Dalton didn't plan on tonight was getting killed.

With lead flying all around, he scanned the night with narrowed eyes, picking out the rustlers scattered throughout the darkness, trading shots with the ranch hands. Dalton chose a target, moved closer, and took aim. He waited for a flash in the darkness and then took the rustler out with one shot.

Hearing heavy hoof beats, he whirled, Winchester ready. A rider, tall and large-boned, with shaggy black hair and an untrimmed mustache, came galloping from the shadows straight for him. Dalton squeezed off a shot, recognizing the rustler as one of the two remaining Kansas marauders.

The sound spooked the horse, causing it to rear up. The bullet ripped through the animal's neck and brought it to the ground. The rustler rolled away, seeking cover, leaving the squealing animal to die.

Several more riders came from the shadows, bullets flying. As one drew closer, a fierce anger built in Dalton; it was Morgan. The downed rustler grabbed the big man's outstretched hand and jumped on the back of the horse. Rescue complete, the riders headed back to the shadows.

Dalton fired and missed, letting out a stream of cursing.

Without warning, a sharp crack echoed through the air—a rifle shot fired from somewhere behind him. The rustler clinging to Morgan stiffened as the bullet tore into his back. His body tumbled to the hard earth below, lifeless before it hit the ground. Morgan galloped onward, leaving the fallen outlaw sprawled motionless in the dust.

Dalton threw his saddle over one shoulder and ran toward his horse. Ducking as a rifle bullet whizzed past his head, he saddled up and rode into the night, Colt blasting.

Morgan thought he was safe in southwest Missouri, but he was dead wrong. No one was ever truly safe. Not the good or the bad. Morgan was about to find out that there was no safe place to run to or hide anymore. At the end of the trail, all that awaited him was a slow, painful death.

From the hollows of the Ozark hills, hungry wolves howled, moving like gray ghosts through the silent forest as the last of the Kansas raiders galloped away with shots ringing out behind them. The devil wasn't far behind, and when they met again, there would be hell to pay.

Dalton rode through the night, and each beat of the horse's hooves brought him closer to Morgan's hideout in Stone County. He smirked, recalling the words once spoken to him by a preacher man. "Weak men seek revenge, strong men forgive, and intelligent men ignore the wrong done to them."

Dalton recalled his reply, "Preacher, I am none of those things."

Chapter 28

Stone County Missouri

Dalton tracked the rustlers through the rugged hills, hidden hollers, and thick forest of Stone County until he found what appeared to be an abandoned cabin. Overgrown with a partially collapsed roof and decaying wood covered in moss and vines, he reasoned it wasn't the rustlers' hideout.

Dalton reined in his horse and dismounted. He looked through the shattered window. The inside showed signs of neglect and decay. Expecting to find the shack empty, he was taken by surprise when the door swung wide, and a white-haired man with a rifle trained on him limped out. "Don't come any closer, mister!" he barked.

"Whoa, old-timer," Dalton said, stepping back.

"How'd you find my cabin?" he questioned, eyes searching the woods for any sign of movement.

"I'm after a gang of cattle rustlers. Been on their trail for days but lost their tracks in the woods a ways back."

"A lot of trouble in these here hills, after the war," he explained, lowering the rifle. "A man can't be too careful."

Dalton nodded, waiting for the old man's next move.

"Gilbert Flood," he said, offering his hand. "Who might ya' be?"

"Dalton Parnell," he answered, shaking the extended hand.

"Well, Dalton Parnell, come on in," he invited. Setting the rifle by the door, Gilbert shuffled his way across the one-room cabin and eased himself into an old rocker that had seen better days.

Dalton followed. He sat in the only other chair. His gaze circled the room. A wood stove stood on one side and a bed on the other. A table littered with plates and scraps of leftover food sat in the middle of the room.

The white-haired man rocked back and forth, eyeing his guest in silence. Finally, curiosity got the best of him. He stopped rocking and leaned forward in the chair. "So, who are the men ya' after?"

Dalton waited a moment before answering. He reasoned it was best to keep the story short without revealing too many details. "A man named John Morgan led an attack on the Bar Z

Ranch, killing a man."

When Dalton didn't offer more, Gilbert leaned back in the rocker. He reckoned there was more to the story, but from the hard look in the steel-gray eyes across from him, that was all the young man was willing to share.

Gilbert had no love lost for John Morgan; the man had been nothing but trouble for the people of Stone County ever since he returned from the war. Everyone would be glad to be rid of the lawless bastard once and for all. Mind made up, he said, "Morgan has a hideout just a day's ride from here, hidden on the south side of the hill in Hell Holler."

Getting the information he needed, Dalton stood and started for the door.

"Best stay till morning, not a good idea to ride alone at night in these woods," the old man cautioned.

Taking Gilbert's advice, he sat back down. As the evening wore on, the old man lit a kerosene lantern and, puffing on a pipe, told Dalton about the lawlessness that had taken hold in the county after the war.

Hearing the steady beat of horses galloping towards the cabin, the old man grew silent. He blew out the lamp and reached for his rifle.

Dalton drew his guns and raced to the window. Riders circled the cabin faces hidden by masks stitched from burlap and gunny sacks. The men carried lanterns, pistols at their hips, and shotguns slung over broad shoulders.

"Bald Knobbers!" the old man yelled at Dalton from the other window. They're not here to rob; they've come because they think I'm in cahoots with a band of bootleggers. It's just a rumor, but truth matters little to the Ball Knobbers; suspicion alone is enough."

The leader first struck the door in three thunderous knocks. Silence fell within the cabin. "Open up, Gilbert," he barked, his voice unrecognizable behind the mask. "We've come for justice."

"Come and get me!" the old man yelled.

That was what the men outside were waiting to hear. Whooping and hollering, they let the bullets fly. One pierced the pine wall and hit Dalton in the chest. He groaned and slumped to the floor.

The cabin door burst open. A lone gunman entered and fired, hitting Gilbert in the head. He fell dead next to Dalton. More men entered the cabin. Several Bald Knobbers, their faces obscured by hoods, gripped the limp bodies of Dalton and Gilbert.

They dragged both men from the cabin onto the dirt and stones outside. Dalton, barely conscious, his shirt stained with blood, struggled weakly against their grip, but the Bald Knobbers were relentless.

Under the pale moonlight, a grim procession wound its way across the rocky ground. The men's boots thudded against the earth as they approached an old well at the edge of the clearing. In silence, they tossed the two men in. As the bodies hit the shallow water with a splash, the Bald Knobbers set the cabin ablaze.

With the bootlegging problem solved, the

riders returned the way they had come, vanishing into the trees and brush of the woods.

When a dull ache throbbed through his chest, Dalton came to, his eyes blinking against the morning light. As his vision sharpened, he realized he was lying at the bottom of a cold, dirt-walled well.

For a moment, he lay still, boots scraping against pebbles. He pushed the old man's body aside and sat up, grimacing. He glanced around.

The walls rose steeply and were water-worn. In one corner, there was a battered tin bucket half-buried in the silt. The well was almost dry, save for a muddy pool; he sat in.

Gathering his strength, Dalton struggled to stand. The bullet struck him high on the left side of his chest. Thankfully, the round, intended to put an end to him, met only flesh. Painful, but not deadly, he gently rubbed the wound while studying the walls, searching for a foothold.

With a deep breath, he launched himself upward, scrambling for a handhold. For every inch gained, he lost half again, sliding down with a rain of loose soil. Sweat stung his eyes, and his breath grew ragged, but he pressed on.

Gripping, scrambling, hauling himself higher. Inch by inch, he clawed his way upward until he reached the top, heaved himself over the rim, and collapsed in a tangle of limbs.

Over the next few weeks, he stuck close to the burnt-out cabin, giving his wound time to heal. His horse, skittish but not injured, returned. He dug what he could from the ashes, hunted for food, and drank water from a nearby creek.

With each passing day, he grew stronger until he was finally able to mount the gelding and ride out. Thanks to Gilbert Flood, he finally knew where to find the last Kansas marauder.

Chapter 29

Stone County Missouri

After riding south for some time, Dalton had just about given up when he drew upon a ridge that looked down on what he was searching for, Morgan's hideout. *The remoteness probably added to its appeal for the outlaw,"* Dalton surmised.

On his search, he had followed a trail that took him through thick stands of sassafras, cedar, and oak in Stone County, Missouri. It was a maze of steep hills, sharp ridges, and streams with chert-clogged channels. *If you break the law and don't want to get caught, this would be a good place to hide,* Dalton reasoned.

He casually took the sack of tobacco and packet of rolling papers from his vest pocket. Peeling off one of the thin sheets, Dalton rolled a cigarette and lit it. He took a drag. Shaking out the match, he dropped it to the ground.

He studied the weather-beaten shack and dilapidated barn as he enjoyed his cigarette. Smoke wafting from the old, crumbling chimney signaled someone was inside. No horses tethered out front at the hitch or loose in the paddock made Dalton think he had missed John Morgan and his band of outlaws. But maybe he could leave a message for the big man... one that a ruthless murderer like Morgan could understand.

He tossed the butt and slowly rode down the steep hillside to the homestead. As he reached the yard, a young man stepped from the shadows of the barn with a shotgun folded in his crossed arms.

"Who are ya, mister?"

"I'm a stranger. You don't know me."

"Well, what do ya want?"

"I'm looking for John Morgan."

A worn-looking woman with a pistol at her side stepped to the doorway of the shack, shielding someone behind her. "What do ya want with my husband?" she asked, voice gruff and demanding.

"Well, ma'am, I intend to kill him," Dalton replied politely, voice cold and stare even colder.

Not liking the answer, the boy and the woman both leveled their guns at the lone rider. Dalton reacted to the threat with a quick draw and three shots. The first sent the boy backward, dead before he hit the ground.

The second spun the woman around. She crumpled to the floor with a groan. As she fell,

Dalton fired his last shot. The light from the fireplace played over the bodies and the pooling blood. The woman was dead, but a small boy lay beside her, holding his cheek, bleeding and moaning.

Dalton started to dismount to finish the job, but then hesitated. *What satisfaction will come from slaying a child?* he reasoned. Reining his mount, he rode back the way he came. He figured the nearest town was at least a day's ride.

Chapter 30

Ozark, Missouri

"**Any** last words?" Sheriff Zacharis Johnson asked the four handcuffed men standing on the scaffold platform. The end of the Civil War had brought dangerous men to southern Missouri and northern Arkansas; men who had cut their teeth on killing. It brought men like John Morgan and vigilante groups like the Bald Knobbers. The sheriff's job was to bring the lawless to justice.

Morgan defiantly stared at the spectators jostling to get a better view. Finally coming to the realization, it was the end for him, he spat and cried out, "Get it over with!"

Dalton watched the proceedings with interest. He thought back over what had led up to this moment. He had arrived in the Christian County town of Ozark shortly after first reading about the Bald Knobbers in the *Kansas City Star*. More than eighty members of the vigilante group, including John Morgan, were charged with crimes from unlawful assembly to first-degree murder.

The group had been terrorizing the hills and hollers of the Ozark Mountains for years. Their distinctive hoods, designed to strike fear in their victims, were made of cloth bags with the top two ends dyed red and tied to look like horns.

Best he could figure from the newspaper account, the Civil War was being reenacted in the Ozarks. The newspaper claimed the Bald Knobbers were ex-Union soldiers, now businessmen.

The original group was said to be about a dozen and went by different names, but the one that stuck was the "Bald Knobbers," given because the group met in open, bald spaces on the top of the area's prominent hills, called "knobs."

The other side tended to be ex-Confederates and long-term residents, most farmed for a living. The businessmen looked down on these native "hill men" as backward.

Over the years, it was unclear how many died in the fighting between the two groups. The reporter's estimates ranged from a dozen to more than thirty, with countless more beaten and driven from their land.

Governor Marmaduke, who, strangely enough, was a former Confederate general, was quoted in the newspaper, "The lynching, night riding, and shootouts must be stamped out. I don't care who fought for which side; I just want the killing to stop."

The governor got what he wanted with the arrest of eighty Bald Knobbers. The newsworthy story of the indictment and trial appeared on the front page of every paper across the nation, even the prestigious *New York Times*.

Meanwhile, in Ozark, amid an almost carnival-like setting, the inevitable group of loiterers gathered. Some sought comfortable positions on the bench in front of the dry goods store. Others claimed the ground under a tree near one of the courthouse's open windows.

These men spent hours following the comings and goings at the building. They knew every witness called to testify, every question asked, and every answer given. They prided themselves on accurately retelling every detail to interested listeners, and Dalton was willing to listen.

Dalton remembered sitting under the tree next to one of the old-timers, listening intently to his story. "Well, here's how I heard it told," the old man began, settling back against the tree. "Chieftain of the Bald Knobbers, Dave Walker, called a meeting for the purpose of destroying a moonshine still operating in Chadwick."

Clearing his throat, he continued the tale, "Almost all the Knobbers were there, having given the password to the sentry as they entered the naturally barren top of Snapp's Bald. The roaring fire cast an eerie light upon the masked men. There was not a sound except the crackling of the flames and the occasional nicker of horses and mules.

"Walker demanded that the moonshiner be stopped. After a hearty agreement from all present, the men checked and loaded their pistols, rifles, and shotguns, and then mounted their rides.

"Following single file behind their leader, they left the open area of the bald, down the worn, narrow trail cut through the oaks to the rough road below. There were a few occasional words, but by the time they reached the cabin, they were completely quiet. However, the masked men found no evidence of the still, and Walker called off the raid."

"Yah, and if the raiders had stopped there, they wouldn't be facing the noose now!" added a dark-haired man as he stretched out under the shade tree to hear more of the tale.

In his lazy drawl, the old man continued his story, "After Walker left, some of the younger and rowdier members of the vigilante group decided to go off on their own and pay a visit to William Eden, who had often spoken out against the Bald Knobbers. Finding the cabin empty, the men decided to ride on to Eden's father's cabin just down the road."

The old-timer paused, rubbed his neck, taking a moment to remember the details of what occurred next at Eden's cabin, then said, "A light from an old kerosene lamp flickered inside the cabin as the riders approached. Hearing the hoofbeats, old man Eden stepped out onto the porch. He carried a loaded shotgun with him."

"'Who is it?' Eden asked the hooded men.

"A muffled voice answered, 'We're the Bald Knobbers, law in these here hills.'

"'What do you'uns want?' Eden challenged as he raised the shotgun to his shoulder.

"'We're going to teach you to keep your big mouth shut, old man!' the same voice called out.

"Fearing the worst, Eden hurried to get back in the house and bolt the door. It did no good. There were too many of them, and the raiders easily busted open the front door and shot the old man standing in front of them with his shotgun in hand, prepared to defend himself and his family. Then they shot Charley Green, paying a visit to the cabin along with his wife, as well as their intended target, William Eden, also in the cabin.

"One of the more sensible men eventually gained control of the rampaging vigilantes before they shot Mrs. Green. He finally got all of the Bald Knobbers out of the cabin and sent for Dave Walker."

A young man, sounding suspiciously like a Knobber sympathizer, spoke up, "I heard, when Walker got to the cabin and saw the damage, he ordered all of the men to go home."

"I reckon you're right, but it was too late for the three dead men." Dalton pointed out plucking a blade of grass, examining it thoughtfully, and then tossing it aside.

"The way I see it," an elderly listener cut in,

"Dave Walker's as guilty as sin. He didn't pull the trigger this time, but he's been in on plenty of other killin's in these here parts."

Bring his story to an end, the old-timer finished with, "I was sittin' right here the day Sheriff Johnson testified that upon arriving at the Eden cabin, he talked with Mrs. Green. She told him she could identify the son of Dave Walker, William Walker, John Matthews, his nephew Wiley Matthews, and John Morgan, as well as others involved in the massacre. The next morning, the sheriff said he set about arresting the entire group one by one, meeting little resistance."

The day the verdict was announced, Dalton stood outside the courthouse with the elderly storyteller and most of the town's people. A cheer went up inside and outside of the courtroom when the judge sentenced the four to hang. The others were given a range of punishments from $50 fines to several years in the state penitentiary.

"All that's left is the execution," the old-timer said to Dalton before turning and walking to his favorite shade tree. Sitting, he settled back, cupped his hands behind his head, and closed his eyes.

Now, today, a few months later, Dalton stood in the courtyard outside the jail. A throng of hundreds crowded around to get a better view over the fence erected to protect the curious, as well as those responsible for carrying out the punishment. He felt nothing, no hate, no regret, just a numbing emptiness.

"Let's get this over with," the sheriff demanded. This was Johnson's first hanging. He had ordered the carpenter to build the scaffold with four nooses and one large trap door so all the men would be hanged with one drop. Wanting to get it over with as soon as possible, he pulled the lever, and the men fell.

There was a terrible groan from the onlookers. The men, wild with pain, beat and thrashed around. Gurgling and choking, they twisted to-and-fro, striking against each other, legs intertwining as they struggled in the throes of death.

For fifteen minutes, the crowd stood in silence. Finally, all signs of life disappeared from the bodies.

So ends John Morgan's reign of terror, Dalton thought. It was fitting that Morgan's death was as agonizing and violent as the crimes he had brought on the helpless people of Kansas and Missouri.

Dalton turned and walked to his horse tied to a hitch in front of the dry goods store. He swung up into the saddle, reined the gelding to the west, and made for Dodge City, Kansas.

Justice had been served; the last man on his list now faced his Maker, where the ultimate punishment awaited: a second death—the "lake of fire."

CHAPTER 31

Dodge City, Kansas

Dalton already had a history by the time he got to Dodge. He had nothing to live for and didn't make it a secret. There was a certain freedom; however, when you think your life is over.

Once, driven by a singular purpose: to hunt down and kill every man responsible for a great wrong. But as the last target fell, the burning drive that had sustained him for years faded. His purpose was gone, no revenge to fuel him, Dalton became a shadow passing through town after town.

For several years, he took on jobs—sometimes as a ranch hand, sometimes as a bartender, occasionally as a hired gun for those desperate enough not to ask about his past. Each town offered a chance at a new beginning, but none held enough promise or comfort to keep him rooted.

The atmosphere in the Long Branch Saloon was tense with the potential for violence. All the men around the table sat stiffly, waiting for the next turn of cards and the trouble it might bring, except for Dalton.

Stetson tipped back, a smile on his face; he regarded the cards in front of him: two jacks and a deuce. He picked up some bills from the pile next to him and tossed the paper into the center of the table with the rest of the pot. "I'll see that ten and raise twenty."

Most of the other players had already folded as the pot grew. The player to his left muttered, "Forget it," shoved his chair away from the table, and headed for the bar.

Dalton stared across the green felt at the young man... John Morgan's son. With dark hair and a narrow mustache, his battered hat hung behind his head from its chin strap. Dalton said, "Looks like it's down to you and me, Kid."

The young man's pile of winnings had grown considerably smaller over the course of the night. He hesitated, rubbed the deep scar that marked his cheek, then picked up some bills and tossed them into the pot. "There's your damn twenty!"

The nervous-looking dealer swallowed, cleared his throat, and dealt a card face up to Dalton. "That's a seven," he announced unnecessarily since everybody could see what the card was. "Still a pair of jacks showing."

With expert skill, he flipped the next card in the deck to the kid. "An eight. That gives you two-pair, black Aces and black eights."

"We can all see that; damn it!" the kid snapped.

Dalton let out a low whistle. "Dead Man's Hand! Aces and eights, the same five-card stud hand Hickok held when shot in the back of the head by that coward Jack McCall."

The dealer, like most gamblers, was superstitious; he cautioned, "Hey, mister, speaking of the dead is bad luck!"

The young gambler saw through the cheap trick to rile him up and cause trouble. Too late, Lady Luck was on his side tonight. Unafraid, refusing to take the bait, he looked the cowboy in the eye. "Who the hell bids up the pot on a lousy pair of jacks? It's not good enough to beat me, and ya know it."

Dalton smiled in response. Experience had taught him that the people who have the cards are usually the ones who talk the least and the softest; those who are bluffing tend to talk loudly and give themselves away.

The young man's mouth flattened; his eyes went hard, "I know who ya are. A damn tinhorn gambler who should've been run out of town by now."

The grin on Dalton's face didn't budge, but his eyes turned hard as flint. "This game has been dealt fair and square." He put his hand on the pile of bills to his left and pushed it into the middle of the table. "And I reckon I'm all in." Dalton settled back into his seat.

"I'm not goin' to let ya bluff me!" The kid pushed his remaining money into the pile at the center of the table. "I'm goin' to call, ya."

He turned over his hole card, which was a seven. "My aces and eights beat your two jacks," he announced, reaching for the pot.

"Hold on," Dalton demanded, flipping over his hole card, a jack. "Three of a kind always beats two-pair."

The kid's face grew dark with anger as he stared at the cards. His breath hissed between clenched teeth. He angrily shoved his chair back and stood.

Dalton's right hand moved closer to the gun at his hip. Everybody in the saloon started edging away. The lace and fringed serving girls ducked behind cover. In a matter of moments, nobody was anywhere near the two players.

The kid uttered a curse and clawed the six-shooter at his hip. He started to lift the gun—only to stop short as he found himself staring down the barrel of Dalton's Colt.

Dalton advised, "Saddle your horse and ride on out. Hanging around here is going to get you killed!"

Slowly replacing his gun, hands held to his sides, the young gambler backed from the saloon.

Dalton slugged back his drink while scooping the bills from the table. Scrapping the chair back, he stood and stuffed the winnings in a pocket. He walked out into the night, leaving the batwing doors swinging.

Across the street, three men watched. And,

when he started down the wooden boardwalk, they marched along keeping pace with him from the other side. One was the kid. Dalton paid them no mind and kept walking. It was obvious where he was headed. At the end of the street was the livery, and beyond, nothing else.

At the livery, he stopped. The three men stopped. Dalton stepped off the boardwalk and onto the dirt street. He walked straight across toward the three men.

"I want my money!" the kid shouted.

Dalton kept walking. The kid hadn't expected that. He wasn't sure what he should do.

"Hey, mister, what the hell ya' doin'?" he asked.

"I'm going to kill you all," Dalton said. He didn't speak very loudly, but the three heard, and his steady voice made them flinch back a half step.

Dalton could feel the steady rhythm of his heart. He felt the weight of the Colts in his belt. He opened his hands wide and let them relax at his sides. He was close now. If the kid was going to make his move, he'd need to do it soon, before Dalton was on top of him. The kid knew it and went for his gun.

With one fluid motion, Dalton drew and fired, the Colt bucking slightly as the hammer fell. The shot hit Morgan's son before his hand reached the butt of the six-shooter.

One of the young gambler's friends managed to get a shot off, hitting Dalton in the right arm. Without any pause, Dalton shot the two men.

Then there was silence. In the utter stillness, the smell of gunpowder was thick. Dalton reloaded and walked to each man to make sure they were dead. Holstering the Colt, he walked on to the livery.

Chapter 32

Beer City, Oklahoma

The woman rode sidesaddle into town, followed by a gang of hard-looking men. She had taken one look at Dalton standing on the balcony of the boarding house and hadn't looked anywhere else. The last rays of the setting sun etched the sternly handsome face, watching her, watching him.

Dalton guessed it was to be expected. Once word got around about the lack of law in Beer City, Oklahoma, it became a magnet for outlaws like them.

He read the message scrawled across the scrap of paper again as his high-heeled boots kicked up dust crossing the street, "Let's talk." He knew the writer. Known to be partial to good whiskey and gambling, he also knew where to find her.

The swinging doors brushed up against Dalton as he entered the Buckhorn Saloon, already crowded with a rowdy, high-spirited mix of cowboys, gamblers, thieves, and fancy women. Walking to the bar, he ordered whiskey. Glass in hand, he turned and cast a wide glance around the room.

Strikingly handsome, she stood out in the amber-yellow glow of the kerosene lanterns. Tight black jacket, black velvet skirt, and twin pistols, with belts of cartridges crisscrossing her hips, Belle Starr, female outlaw, waited.

Swallowing the last of the amber liquid, feeling the burn, he recalled what he had heard about this woman known to the ruthless men she traveled with as the "Bandit Queen."

Her family had been sympathizers with the Southern cause during the war. Supporters of the Confederate irregulars, Belle had strapped on a six-shooter and crossed the Missouri-Kansas line disguised as a man to join Quantrill's raiders. Eventually, after hooking up with Frank and Jesse James, as well as Cole Younger, lawlessness became a means of survival.

After the War, she gained a reputation as an outlaw and a loose woman. Her ranch in Indian Territory west of Fort Smith, Arkansas, became a hideout for rustlers, horse thieves, and bank robbers.

The illegal activities she organized and planned from the remote location proved profitable. When unable to buy off lawmen, she was known to seduce them into looking the other way.

Dalton had to admit the message had set him to wondering. Sliding his glass to the bartender, he made a path through the tables to where she sat. Her men, protective and loyal, tracked his every move.

Belle had seen the lone gunman walk into the saloon. More than six feet tall, the width of his shoulders and the depth of his chest matched his height. Around his lean waist rode a cartridge belt; from the holster protruded the butts of pearl-handled Colts. He looked like a man who was afraid of nothing—a man who could take care of himself.

"Next to a fine horse, I admire a fine pistol," she declared in a low husky voice.

Not to be taken in by her flirty ways, Dalton questioned, "You wanted to see me?"

"I'm look'n for another rider and gun, interested?" she asked, getting down to business.

"Depends," he answered, pulling out a chair and sitting across from her.

"I plan to stop a freight train."

"Why me?" he asked. Scanning the faces of the men watching him, he said, "Looks like you have plenty of help."

"The train is carrying gold brick headed for the Denver Mint. It will be heavily guarded. Need another gun in case of trouble."

"No disrespect, ma'am, but been on my own since I was a kid. Works best that way," he explained, turning down her offer. Pushing back his chair, tipping the black Stetson, he said, “Night, ma’am.” With quick, smooth strides, Dalton left the saloon.

Early the next morning, he raked back the curtain to the boarding house window just in time to see Belle and her men mount up and ride out. Weeks later, he heard that horsemen had flagged down the Missouri and Northern Arkansas train.

After the locomotive came to a halt, two masked men boarded and held guns on the engineer. The others rode up to the railcar holding the gold and ordered the guards to open up. When the men refused, the robbers simply blew the doors off with sticks of dynamite, pushed aside the dazed guards, and took what they wanted.

Before riding away with the loot, the men removed one of the iron doors from a railroad car. Using ropes, they dragged the door along behind them as they made their escape on horseback.

Railroad detectives hunted for weeks but never found the stash of gold bricks.

The way Dalton figured, Belle, fearing immediate pursuit by federal agents, decided to hide the gold. But the part about the door had him scratching his head. The answer came in a flash. Riddled with caves and underground tunnels, the nearby mountain-top town of Eureka Springs, Arkansas, was the perfect hiding place.

He reasoned that when the horsemen arrived, they entered one of the caves and stacked the gold bricks against a wall. The iron door was placed over the entrance, wedged into position, and covered over with rock and brush.

The gang attempted another train robbery a few months later, but this time things didn't go as planned. When the mail car doors rolled back, rifle fire blasted from Pinkerton Detectives hired to protect railroad interests. Bullets whistled, and guns exploded as the robbers returned fire. Caught in the open, nowhere to hide, all of the gang members lay dead or dying when the smoke cleared.

Not long after, Dalton heard Starr was shot to death near Fort Smith, Arkansas, just before her 41st birthday. With her death, no one remained alive who knew the exact location of what had come to be known as the "Lost Iron Door Cache," but Dalton had a good idea where to begin the search.

Chapter 33

Eureka Springs, Arkansas

Dalton traversed the winding trail of the Ozark hillside. Half-hidden in the vast hardwood forest, he rode around hastily built wooden shanties and pitched tents. Summer's late afternoon stirred the song of cicadas, marking the end of a difficult day's journey. At last, horse and rider descended into the narrow valley on the main road leading to Eureka Springs, Arkansas.

Travelers on horseback, others in wagons and buggies, now shared the dirt-packed avenue with him. Many were seeking a miracle in the healing waters of one of the sixty-five natural flowing springs located in and around the town.

Newspaper testimonials credited the "liquid cure" with amazing healing feats. As word of the miraculous waters began to spread, the afflicted flocked to Eureka Springs in such numbers that the town had transformed from an isolated wilderness to a flourishing city in just a few short months.

Dalton was skeptical about the miracles, but perhaps a spring bath would ease his minor injury.

The settlement was abuzz with excitement and activity. He maneuvered his new mount, a young golden palomino, to the cedar hitching rail outside the Silver Palace Saloon.

His face, weathered by a lifetime of hard living, appeared dangerous and uncaring. Casting a glance skyward and silently cursing the sizzling afternoon heat, he surveyed the unfamiliar surroundings.

Women, some with children in tow or accompanied by men, strolled the walkways. Dominated by whitewashed wooden structures, the boomtown boasted a restaurant, dry goods store, blacksmith and livery, a couple of hotels, and a brick-built bank. Good citizens of the town had seen fit to erect a church and barbershop at one end of the street and a newspaper and post office at the other.

Upstanding businessmen of Eureka Springs had not forgotten to provide accommodations pandering to the darker tastes of men of his persuasion. Next to the Silver Palace was Miss Turnbottom's brothel, and further down the street was a gambling hall.

Riding by the sheriff's office, he was quick to note the collection of wanted posters tacked to the wooden planks. Relieved not to find his likeness, he reasoned the Dodge City Peace Commission had not yet issued a warrant after the deadly gunplay that had left his right arm in need of attention.

After dismounting, he wrapped the reins around the hitch. He removed the salt-stained, blackened Stetson, revealing a full head of wavy golden hair. A red bandana wiped beading sweat and fresh trail dust from his sun-darkened face.

He smiled at the thought of easing his thirst with good whiskey. He winced in pain as he shed the light canvas duster. It was a tolerable pain; one he hoped would mend in time.

His thoughts were interrupted. "Need your horse stabled, mister?" the young boy asked.

"Make sure he gets feed and water." The boy pocketed two bits and led the palomino to the nearby livery.

A din of merrymaking rolled out into the street. Browdy bar tunes echoed from a saloon piano, and shrill laughter from women turned into shrieks as a fight erupted and tumbled onto the main street.

Another smile swept across Dalton's face as he cleared the three steps leading to the saloon. This would be the first stop. Dull the pain and cozy up to a fine-looking woman of the establishment.

Guns holstered low on his hips; the smell of sweat, stale beer, and cheap perfume hit him as he gave the batwing doors an inward push. Curious heads turned. Sensing the newcomer posed no immediate threat, they went back to telling lies and swigging liquor.

He scanned the high-quality establishment. In the far-right corner, the piano player pounded out another lively tune. Painted ladies decked out in lace and fringe danced with men starved for female companionship. On the left, an enormous bar spanned half the room. Two bartenders, dressed in black vests with matching bow ties, stood ready to accommodate the booted and spurred trail hands.

Saloon girls, arms and shoulders bare, bodices cut low over ample bosoms, stood talking to men—enticing them to remain, buying drinks, and patronizing the games.

Striding to the bar, his left arm was nestled by the breasts of a young woman. A river of dark red hair streamed down her back.

"Welcome to the Silver Palace, cowboy. How 'bout a drink and a table?" she asked with an inviting look.

"Yes, ma'am, a table in the back would suit me just fine."

Following his request, the woman led Dalton to a table. From habit, he sat with his back to a wall, facing the door to avoid getting surprised by someone looking to dispense their own version of frontier justice.

"Bottle of your best whiskey and a glass, two glasses if you care to join me," he invited.

The brazen-faced redhead, practicing the world's oldest profession, said, "Perhaps later, I've customers to tend to now."

With a wink and a nod, he said, “I sure am thirsty, ma'am, don't know 'bout later.”

“Don't wait too long!” she warned, twirling away from the table. Under the ruffled skirt, the colorful petticoats that barely reached her leather boots were visible. He caught a glimpse of silk stockings held up by garters, which he reasoned were gifts from her admirers. With an exaggerated swaying of ample hips, she weaved a trail to the bar.

Taking out tobacco pouch and papers, he rolled and lit a cigarette. His steel-gray eyes coldly took in the rest of the saloon from behind a cloud of exhaled smoke.

Faro and poker players were stationed at one of the three large tables in the center of the room. Small round tables, like the one he sat at, were scattered throughout and occupied by groups of two or three men engaged in conversation. He didn't recognize anyone, and no one recognized him.

Minutes later, his drink was served. “Here ya go,” she said, placing the bottle and glass in front of him.

Dalton used his left hand to pull some coins from his shirt pocket. “Keep the change.” He poured himself a drink.

“Thanks,” she beamed, “anything else, Darlin'?”

Shaking his head, no, he waved her away. Large hips and red hair, she wasn't his type, and besides, he didn't want or need the distraction.

Sunlight streaked through the fog of tobacco

smoke as he sucked down the amber contents of the glass. He opened his mouth and let out a breath as the slow burn of the liquor washed away the dust.

He sat silently, drinking and watching the rapidly dimming afternoon sky filled with dark, rolling clouds. Forked lightning, brilliant and white-hot, flashed through the blackening heavens. Crackling thunder rippled; the deafening noise engulfed the wooden building.

The storm broke with a hard rain pelting the mountain top town, bouncing off roofs, forming puddles while he carefully weighed his next steps: search the secret tunnels buried deep beneath the town, find the gold, and then head west to Oregon Country.

At the end of the day, the storm finally blew itself out. Alert but feeling the whiskey, Dalton stepped out into the blue tinge of twilight. Saloon doors creaked quietly behind.

Under the cover of darkness, dodging mud holes, he walked a short distance to the Perry House, a four-story hotel complete with white-columned balconies on the second and third floors. A sign on the glass front entry door read "Vacancy."

Glancing back at the deserted street, his eyes scanned the shadows while his right hand instinctively tapped the pearl-handled Colt. Safety assured, he turned back and stepped into the cool sanctuary of the hotel lobby.

Chapter 34

Eureka Springs, Arkansas

Driven by a vision of lush valleys and opportunities beyond the Ozarks, Dalton dedicated days to chasing leads. He sifted through old newspaper clippings and bribed locals for bits of information. He listened to endless stories claiming that the "Outlaw Queen" had hidden the treasure from her last major train robbery somewhere in the s passageways beneath the town.

As midnight crept across the hills, the Perry House sat silent. Dalton slipped from his room and made his way down to the cellar beneath the hotel.

He found the hidden door just where the map indicated, concealed behind a stack of old whiskey crates. He pulled back the latch and eased the door open. He entered, pulling it closed, shutting out the light.

The tunnel was damp, winding beneath the quiet main street. The air was thick with the scent of earth and decay.

Dalton kept the lantern raised, moving slowly, searching every alcove for a sign of hidden fortune. Shadows danced on the walls, and every step echoed through the dark as he went deeper into the maze of tunnels.

With every dead end, his desperation grew, but so did his determination. His mind fixed on Oregon, where forests stretched to the horizon and past sins could be left behind in the foggy mountains. Freedom from his past lay somewhere in the darkness—just beyond the next twist in the tunnel.

Weary of the uneven path, Dalton reached out for the rough limestone wall. He carefully placed one foot in front of the other, following the cold stones with his free hand. For several minutes, he concentrated on navigating the jagged path that lay ahead.

Rounding a bend, Dalton was startled by a glint of metal, a rusted strongbox, half-buried beneath loose stones. He knelt and pried it open, only to find it empty, except for a faded playing card and a cryptic note: "For those who seek more than gold, the real fun lies ahead."

Confused, Dalton tossed the box aside and continued forward. In some areas, he had to stoop to navigate through the passage, while in other sections, the ceiling towered twenty feet overhead.

Brushing aside a tangle of dusty cobwebs, he

froze—voices. He strained to make out the words, but there was nothing more to be heard. He cautiously edged forward until the tunnel ended at a large wooden door.

Listening closely, he caught the sound of laughter and piano music coming from within. As he knocked, one hand instinctively moved to his Colt.

The door opened, and the scent of perfume replaced dank earth. There stood Miss Turnbottom, owner of the most notorious brothel in town. "Welcome, cowboy, she said, eyeing him with a knowing look.

Dalton couldn't help but smile at the turn of events. "Howdy, ma'am," he said, stepping into the parlor.

Lanterns bathed the room in golden light. The plush chairs, velvet curtains, and ornate mirrors created an atmosphere of luxury far removed from the grimy tunnels. Cowboys and patrons sat playing cards, drinking whiskey, or chatting with the women. The piano player provided entertainment, and the atmosphere was a mix of excitement, relaxation, and occasional rowdiness.

Miss Turnbottom offered Dalton a drink as he watched the "soiled doves" work the room with practiced grace. Dressed in vibrant finery meant to dazzle under the flickering lights, they leaned against ornate banisters, lounged on plush settees, and cast knowing glances toward him, the latest cowboy to enter through the secret tunnel door.

Eager for his attention, the women

employed a mixture of charm and boldness. One, catching his attention, twirled tendrils of blond hair around a gloved finger, her lips curling into a sultry smile. Nearby, another let out a musical laugh, tossing her head so that her dark curls shimmered in the lamp glow.

A third approached with boldness, trailing a finger along Dalton's sleeve as she offered him a drink, her tone teasing and playful. She asked, "Looking for some company tonight, mister?"

Weary from nights of searching and hungry for company, all thoughts of hidden treasure and Oregon Country faded. Dalton grabbed the woman's hand and stood.

"Come on, cowboy," she insisted. Smiling, knowing that look, she led her first customer of the night to a private room upstairs.

Chapter 35

Eureka Springs, Arkansas

He was sitting in the hotel lobby the first time he saw her. Hearing the hoofbeats and the rattle of stagecoach wheels approaching, he looked up from his newspaper and out the window. The coach swayed and bounced up and down along the bumpy dirt street.

"Whoa!" cried the driver. The coach slowed and then stopped in front of the sixty-room Perry House, the most up-to-date and fashionable hostelry in Eureka Springs. "Easy now," he cautioned the six quivering and snorting horses.

Setting the brake, he looped the reins around the handle and then climbed down to the street some seven feet below. He opened the coach door and offered a helping hand to one of the two passengers.

A gloved hand accepted his offer. Gathering her skirt with the other, the young woman carefully stepped down to the street, revealing a slim ankle. She pushed back a strand of honey-blonde hair and then straightened her hat.

While brushing the dust from her skirt, the driver swung a small girl dressed in yellow from the coach, setting her long, cornsilk-colored braids swinging.

The man riding shotgun tossed the woman's trunk to the hotel porter as the driver climbed back to his seat. He snapped the reins over the backs of the horses. Then yelled, "Yee-ah!" The stagecoach lurched and rolled on.

Dalton watched the woman smile down at the child and gently take the small hand in hers. The two entered the hotel and walked to the registration desk.

A damn good-looking woman, Dalton thought. *Fair skin, slender waist, and nicely rounded breasts*. Dalton was quick to note that he wasn't the only male following the sway of the woman's hips in the full skirt as she swept through the lobby and up the stairs with the child.

Dalton stood, stretched, and then, making up his mind, headed for the stairs. Keeping his distance, not wanting to cause alarm, he followed. Rounding the corner of the third floor, he almost collided with the young girl. The mother, struggling with the gold room key, looked up.

The kid's gaze fastened on Dalton's guns.

"Are you an outlaw?" she inquired bluntly.

"I used to be," he answered, surprising her.

"My goodness," the woman remarked, pulling her daughter close. In the glow of the gaslights, guns riding low on his hips, gunslinger fashion, he looked dangerous.

"You're safe with me, ma'am," he assured her. "Let me help you with the door."

She hesitated and then handed over the key. Dalton stepped close, leaving little space between them. He caught the scent of her... fresh and womanly as he accepted the key.

She blushed. For a moment, she thought he was going to kiss her, his face so very close to hers, but he didn't.

Steel-grey eyes glinted with mischief as the lock clicked, and Dalton pushed the door open. He stood back politely, allowing the woman to guide the young child into the room. He wanted to reach out and touch the smooth skin of the woman's cheek with the back of his fingers; he held back, not wanting to frighten her with the bold move.

Turning to face him, she simply said, "Thank you."

"Goodnight, ma'am," Dalton replied, tipping his hat and flashing a grin.

She blushed again, oddly flustered.

As Dalton walked further down the hall to room 310, he considered the fire he glimpsed in the woman's eyes before she closed and locked the door. He wondered, *What kind of man would let a woman like that wander so far from home?*

Dalton took it slow and easy over the next few weeks. First, he found out from the desk clerk, Mrs. Elisabeth Stanly, and her daughter, Sarah, were from back East. Next, he made a point of being around when the two ventured from their room. Meeting in the hallway or in passing on the stairs, Dalton would tip his hat with a smile that never failed to bring a hint of pink to pale cheeks.

Today, he found Elisabeth sitting in the lobby with Sarah at her side. He stopped thinking of her as Mrs. Stanly days ago, which, in his mind, made it easier for him to justify his intentions.

He decided today was the time to make his move. He confidently strolled to the settee across from the easy chair where she sat.

"Good morning, ma'am," he said, casually picking up and opening the discarded newspaper before sitting. Scanning the page, he pretended interest in what he found there.

"Good morning," she replied, taking a sip from the China cup.

"We're going to the bathhouse at 10 o'clock," Sarah announced, leaving her mother's side to sit on the red velvet cushion next to him. Young and innocent, she had come to trust the friendly man with the guns. "I was sick all winter, and Dr. Goodman says the water will help me get my strength back."

Dalton set his paper aside. His fingers fished around and finally pulled the silver timepiece from his vest pocket. Curious, the child leaned close to get a better look. Dalton smiled, snapping the lid and replacing the watch. He announced, “It’s almost time for your bath, little one.”

“There are some pretty rowdy strangers in town right now,” he said, turning his gaze on Elizabeth. “May I escort you and Sarah?”

Taken by surprise, the woman hesitated before answering, “How do you know my name, mister?”

“Dalton... Dalton Parnell from Missouri, ma’am.” He introduced himself with a tip of his Stetson, then explained how he discovered her name. “Desk clerk. He’s a real obliging feller for the right price,” he explained, standing and putting out his hand.

Elisabeth considered the offer. She felt safe with this man, even though she knew from the guns on his hips and his direct manner that he was very dangerous. It might not be a bad thing to have him at her side if there was trouble.

“Very well... Mr. Parnell,” she agreed, taking his outstretched hand and rising from the chair. Conscious of the warm sensation of her hand in his strong calloused one, she shyly tugged free.

Elizabeth briefly looked down on her daughter, still seated, then turned her clear blue eyes on him. “Sarah and I would very much like for you to accompany us this morning,” she said, tenderly replacing his hand with that of her daughter’s smaller one.

In that moment, something inside Dalton changed. The numbness he felt gave way to yearning... a longing for this woman and for a different kind of life. One without violence, vengeance, or retribution.

Chapter 36

Eureka Springs, Arkansas

Dalton paused at the Basin Spring Park arched gateway. A smile curved his lips as he tucked her arm around his. They began their evening stroll in silence. The cobblestones wove a path through lush greenery.

The summer breeze died, leaves ceased to rustle, and even the rumble of wagon wheels and the beat of horse hooves was absent. For the next few moments, the focus of his attention was the crunch of dried twigs beneath his boot heels.

His feelings for her had caused him to ponder his life. *Who am I? What have I become: outlaw, gunfighter, cold-blooded killer?* Although he was unsure of the answers, he was sure of one thing: the innocent boy of his childhood had been slain by ruthless marauders and left to rot on the Kansas prairie.

The wound went deep. In the depths of horror and despair, the darkened path was the one he chose. Over time, the ache of loss and loneliness became part of him, and no amount of hate or revenge was able to drive out the darkness.

Then she came into his world. She brought light to the darkness that welled up within him. She filled up the profound emptiness. If he could stop life for a while, he would stop here; he found, quite to his surprise, that he was happy.

He smiled, transforming the harsh plains of his face. In that moment, Dalton realized the greatest thing in life was to love and to be loved in return.

Dalton had his mind set on her, but it would take money. He was more determined than ever to find the Banded Queen's stash of gold; he just needed a little more time.

He paused under the low-hanging branches of an oak tree and turned to her. She stared up at him, caught by the color of his eyes, steel-gray, startling against the sunbaked face. Crisp blond hair curled out from beneath the rim of his dark Stetson.

The white linen shirt tucked into denim pants did little to conceal the male strength of his body. From his waist hung a gun belt with pearl-handled Colts strapped to his hips.

Dalton measured her for an unsmiling moment, then nodded abruptly. "Still want to come with me?"

"Yes," she answered quickly.

His long finger tilted her chin up.

She met his eyes without blinking.

Slowly, he bent to take her lips. Gently, he moved over her mouth. His arms closed around her slender waist while he kissed her with hunger as deep as the spring that ran beneath the park. When he finally lifted his mouth, he searched her face, breathing deep.

At last, voice husky, almost hard, he said, "Alright."

Chapter 37

Eureka Springs, Arkansas

"**Fire**! Fire!" The alarm sounded up and down the hall.

When Dalton woke, he was disoriented, not understanding. He barely remembered falling asleep. After an afternoon of searching the tunnels and a night of drinking and gambling, he stumbled to bed, not even removing his boots.

The first thing he noticed was the yellow-orange glow coming from the window. Jumping up, he checked his timepiece; the hands pointed straight up. Midnight, he noted, yanking back the curtain. "What the hell?"

Fire was everywhere; it was devouring everything in its path. In hopes of saving the screaming horses trapped in the stable, someone had opened the doors and driven them into the street. Dalton was relieved that his golden palomino was one of the animals he saw racing for safety.

"Oh, God... no!" he begged in desperation as he watched the destruction of the town. The tightly packed wooden structures could not withstand the red and yellow fury sweeping through the streets.

Quicker and quicker the infernos advanced, gaining strength. As Dalton turned from the horrific scene, the Perry House was engulfed in a blazing inferno.

"Elizabeth... Sarah!" he whispered with a gut-wrenching groan.

His body exploded into action. He strapped on the Colts and struggled into the white canvas duster. He would need extra protection against what awaited him in the hall.

Grabbing the Stetson from the bed, he opened the door to chaos. The screams and cries of the women mingled with the wailing of children and the shouts of men.

Black smoke billowed into the heated air, so thick that it was difficult to breathe. Flames leaped and danced, terrorizing half-dressed guests fleeing their rooms while orange blazes blew out windows, sending red horizontal jets out into the night.

The burn is too quick and too ferocious for the firefighters to get here in time. Nobody will likely survive, he thought. Dalton knew if he didn't want to be trapped in this burning hellhole, he would have to fight his way through the smoky firestorm.

Grim-faced, he tugged the bandanna from his neck up, covering mouth and nose. He groped his way through the fog of smoke for what seemed like an eternity, finally reaching Elizabeth's room.

She answered his pounding, in a white dressing gown with Sarah at her side. Hair loose about her shoulders and panic in her eyes, she went willingly into his arms.

He briefly brushed his lips across her temple and then bent and scooped up the child. Her arms wrapped tightly around his neck as she buried her small, frightened face in his shoulder. Grabbing Elizabeth tight around the waist, he headed for the stairs.

Please, this can't be the end, not when I've just found something worth living for, he silently prayed as smoke and ash rained down into their hair and eyes. But it was too late; flames were already greedily licking at the walls and blocking any chance of escape.

Fire beat them back, the heat so intense that it threatened to burn lungs and scorch flesh. He had a vague sense of disbelief, a feeling of betrayal, when, with a crash, the third-floor roof groaned and then fell in on them.

Holding Elizabeth and Sarah close, the three disappeared in a cloud of smoke and burning timber.

Epilogue

In those final minutes, amid the roaring chaos of collapsing beams and suffocating smoke, Dalton's thoughts became eerily clear. His mind drifted, not to regret nor unfinished business, but to a memory from years past—a preacher's solemn voice echoing through a humble chapel: "No one knows when their day or hour will come, but no one escapes the call of death. Some come to terms with it. They do not fear the end. Their affairs are in order, and they've made peace with their Creator."

Those words, spoken softly long ago, thundered through Dalton's heart as the floor trembled beneath his feet. He understood them now in a way he never had before.

He wasn't afraid; instead, a strange acceptance settled over him. The preacher's warning had always sounded distant, intended for someone else. Now, in the furnace of his ending, it belonged to him.

AUTHORS' NOTE

Although the events in this novel are fictional, they're loosely based on incidents that occurred during the 1800s and focus on an area known as the Lawless Ozarks, including Missouri and Arkansas.

Missouri earned the title "Outlaw State" because it served as a refuge for many infamous outlaws, such as Jesse and Frank James, the Younger brothers, and Belle Starr, especially during and after the Civil War. Seen as common criminals by some and Robin Hoods with six-shooters by others, the Missouri outlaws left a lasting mark on American culture. These notorious bandits have become folk legends in numerous books, movies, and television shows.

Throughout the outlaw era, Arkansas attracted many infamous criminals due to its numerous caves and rugged terrain, which offered ideal hiding spots for Missouri bandits looking to evade capture.

The boomtown of Eureka Springs became

particularly appealing, featuring seventeen saloons that catered to the outlaws with activities such as gambling, drinking, and prostitution. Notable figures such as Frank and Jesse James, Cole Younger, Belle Starr, and members of the Dalton Gang were known to frequent the area during this time.

According to local history, the elegant four-story Perry House Hotel was built in Eureka Springs in 1880. Like many other buildings in the area at that time, the Perry House was constructed entirely of wood.

Unfortunately, it was consumed by the last of four major fires that devastated the town in 1890. In 1905, William Duncan built the Basin Park Hotel from local limestone on the site where the Perry House once stood.

Legend has it that guests who stay in rooms on the third floor of the Basin Park Hotel frequently report encounters with a young translucent woman with blue eyes and golden-blonde hair, a little girl wearing a yellow dress with braided hair, and a man dressed in a cowboy hat and a white canvas duster, complete with six-shooters strapped to his hips.

The cowboy is said to walk through the walls of the third-floor rooms, asking startled guests if they have seen his horse. Additionally, management often receives late-night reports of shouts of "Fire!" echoing through the hotel.

About the Author

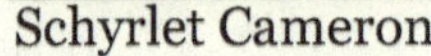

Schyrlet Cameron Kathy Brown

CC Brown is the pseudonym adopted by two sisters, Schyrlet Cameron and Kathy Brown. Growing up in southwest Missouri, they developed a curiosity about the good men and bad men who ruled the Lawless Ozarks, sparked by their grandmother.

As children, they spent much of their time on their grandparents' farm, where their grandmother always kept them entertained by tending the garden, feeding chickens, milking cows, and telling late-night tales of bandits, outlaws, gunslingers, and the lawmen who brought them to justice. Their fascination with the history of the Ozarks has not diminished over time.

www.ingramcontent.com/pod-product-compliance
Lightning Source LLC
LaVergne TN
LVHW090944080826
845145LV00003B/879

* 9 7 8 1 9 7 0 5 6 0 1 9 0 *